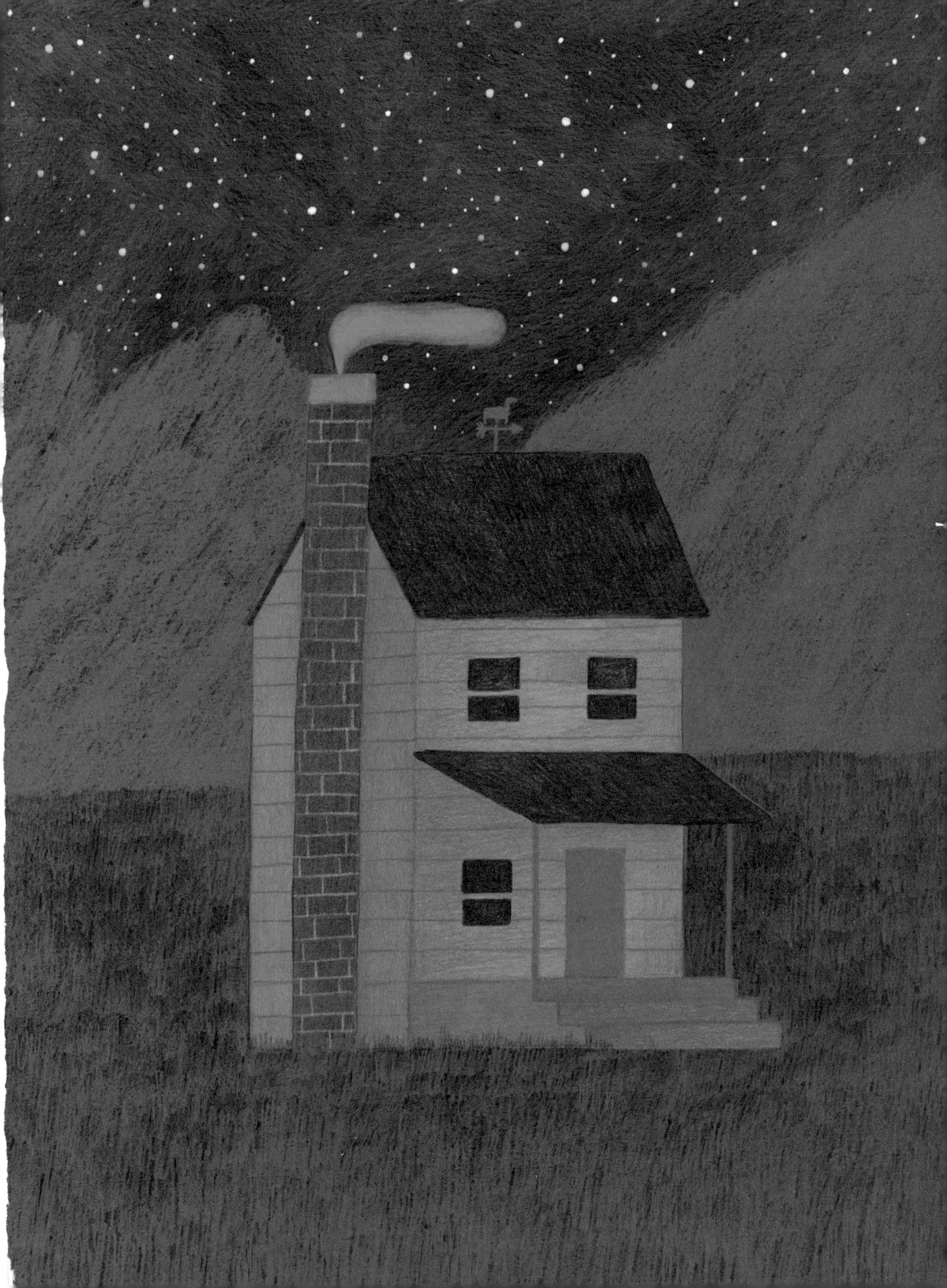

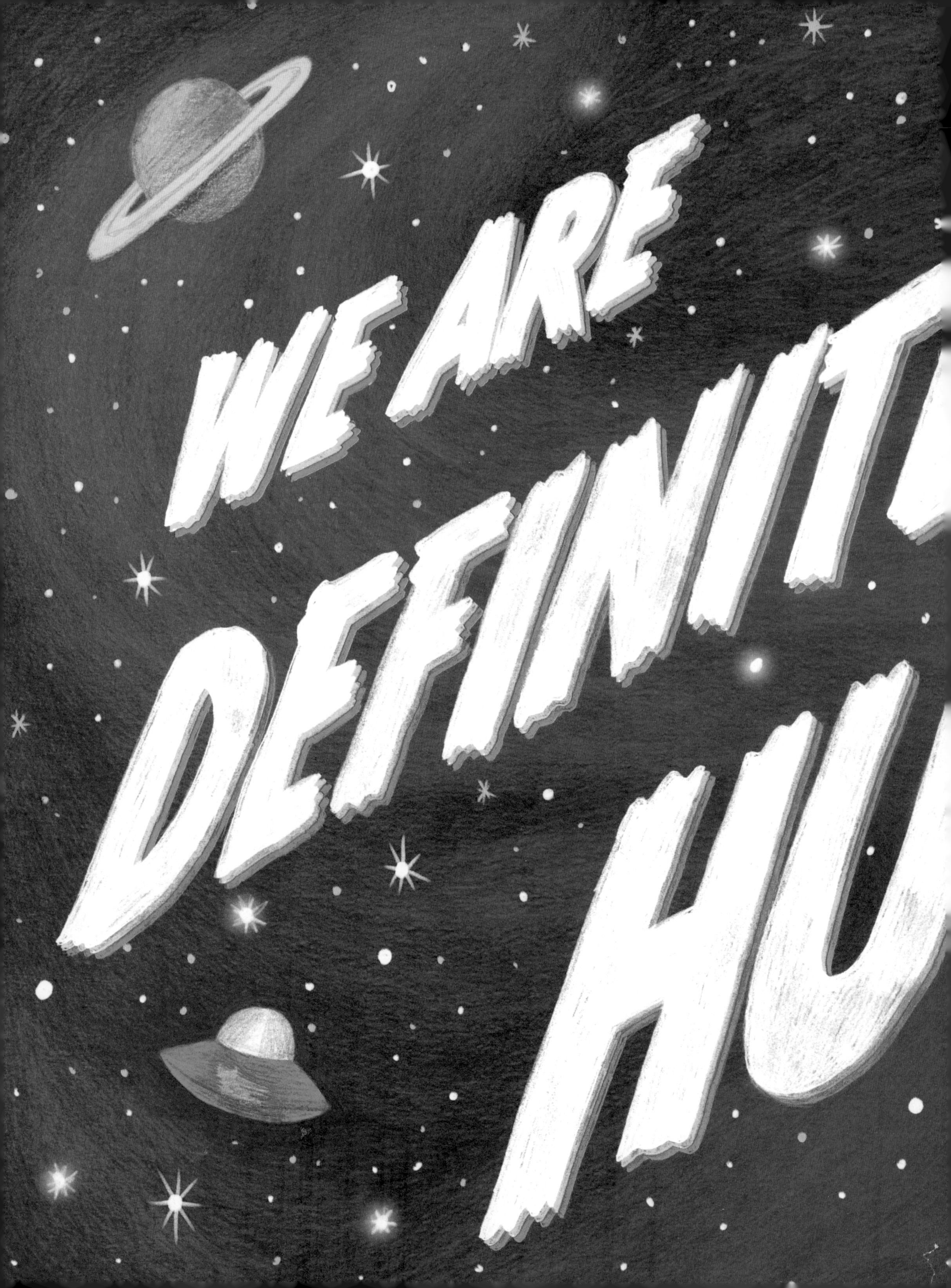
WE ARE
DEFINIT
HU

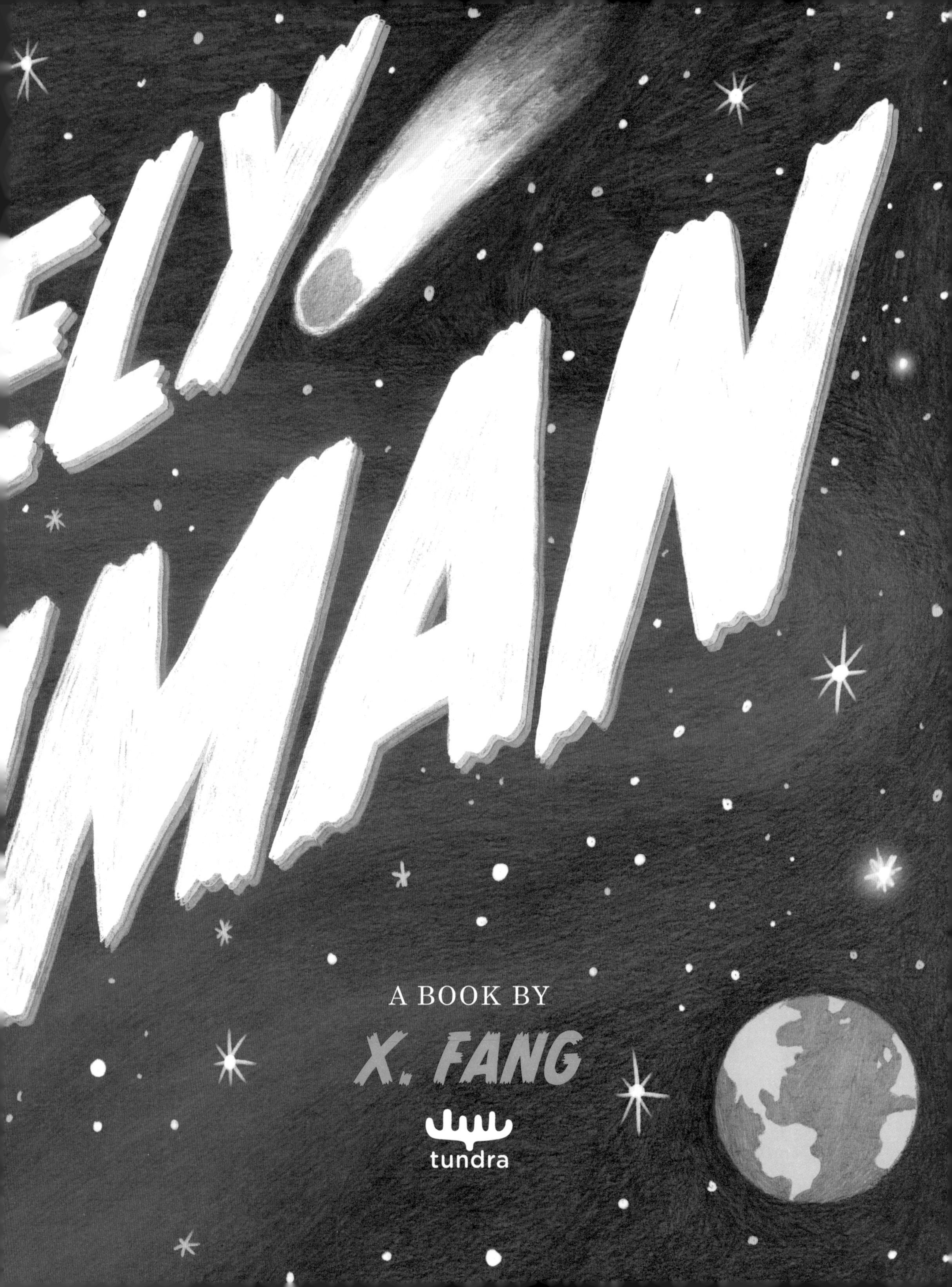
ELY
MAN

A BOOK BY

X. FANG

tundra

It was midnight when
something crashed outside
Mr. and Mrs. Li's house.

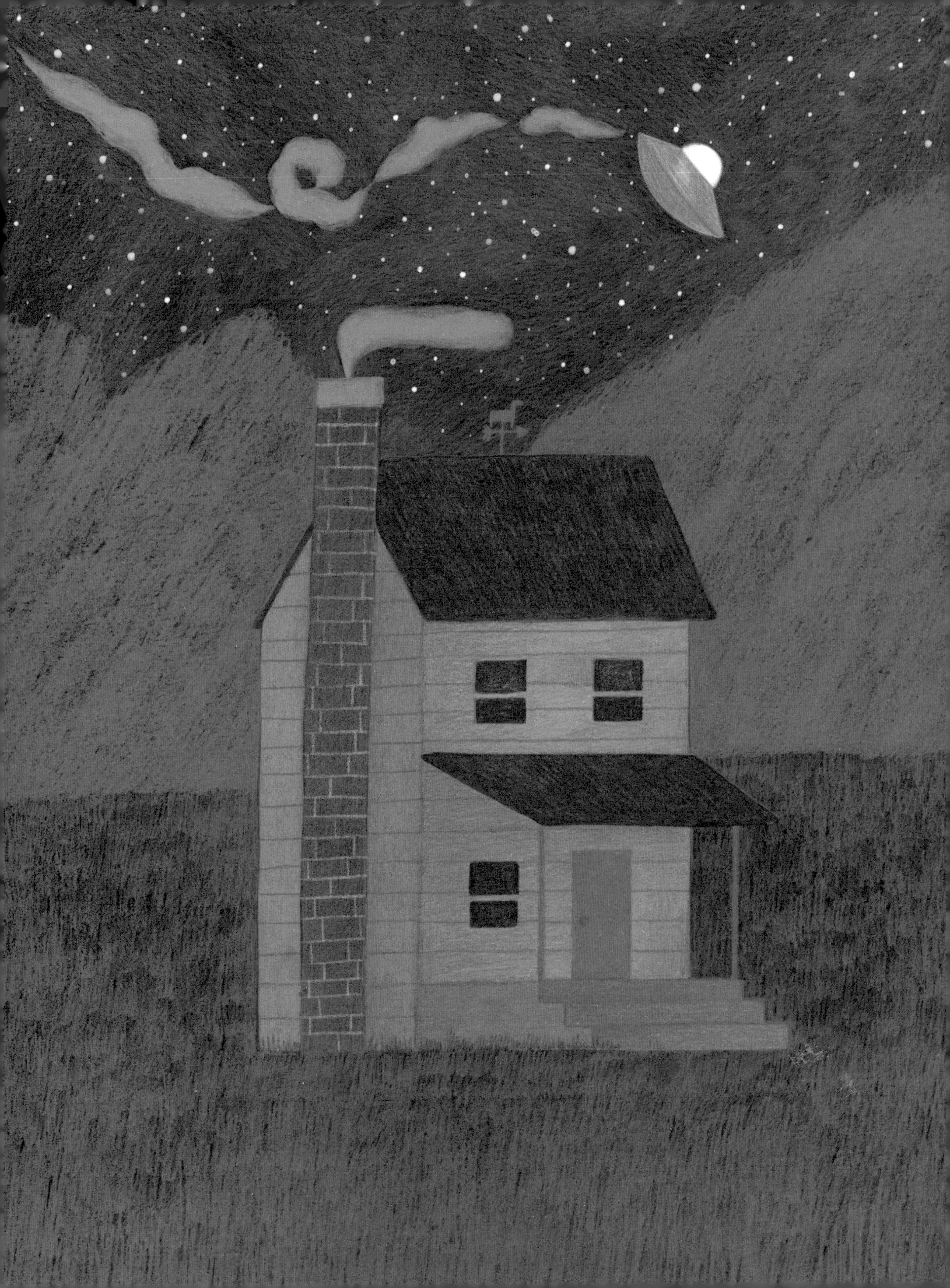

The crash was so loud,
it immediately woke Mr. Li.

"What was that?!" he shouted.

Mrs. Li, however, was sound asleep
and snoring very loudly.

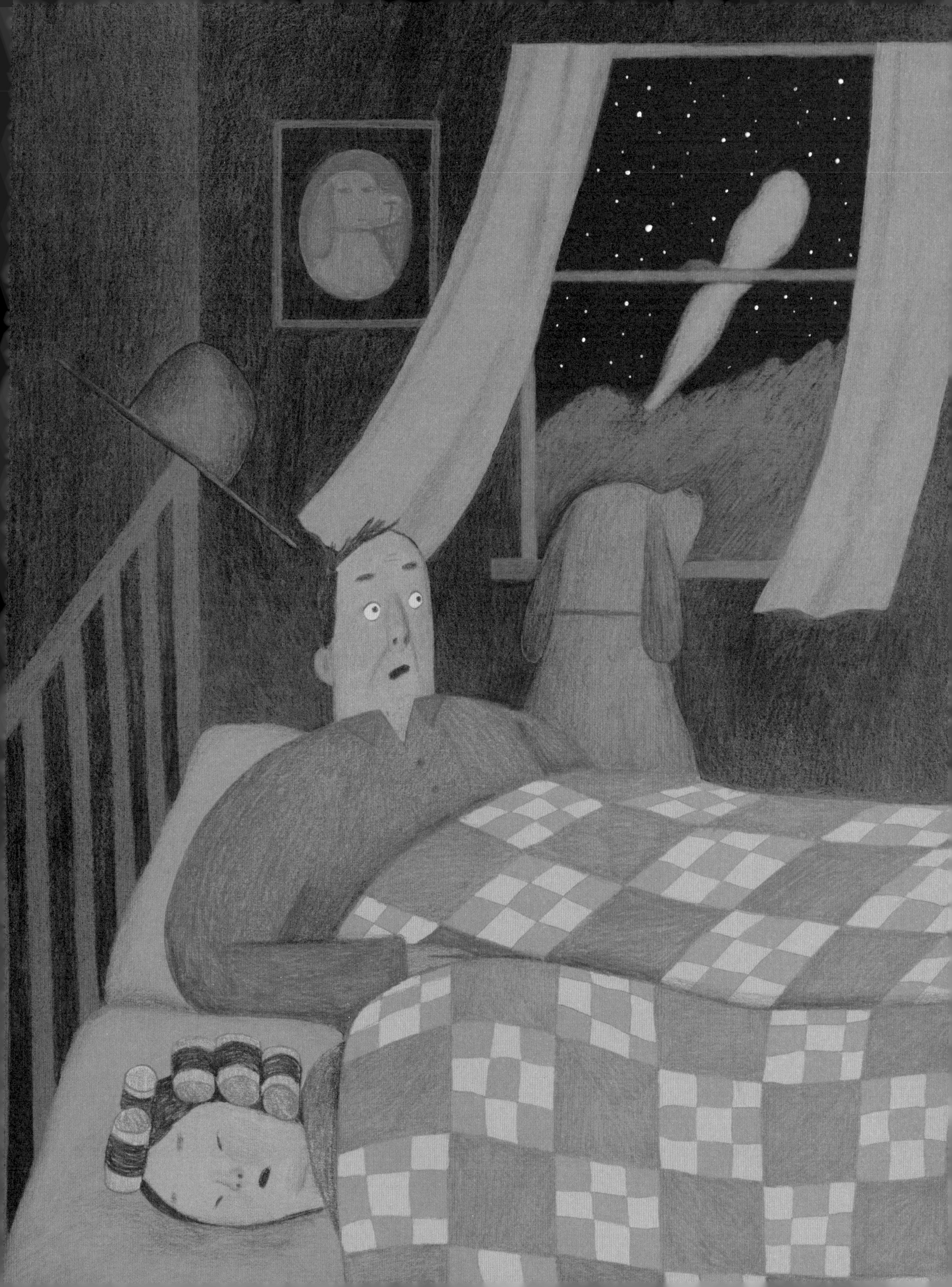

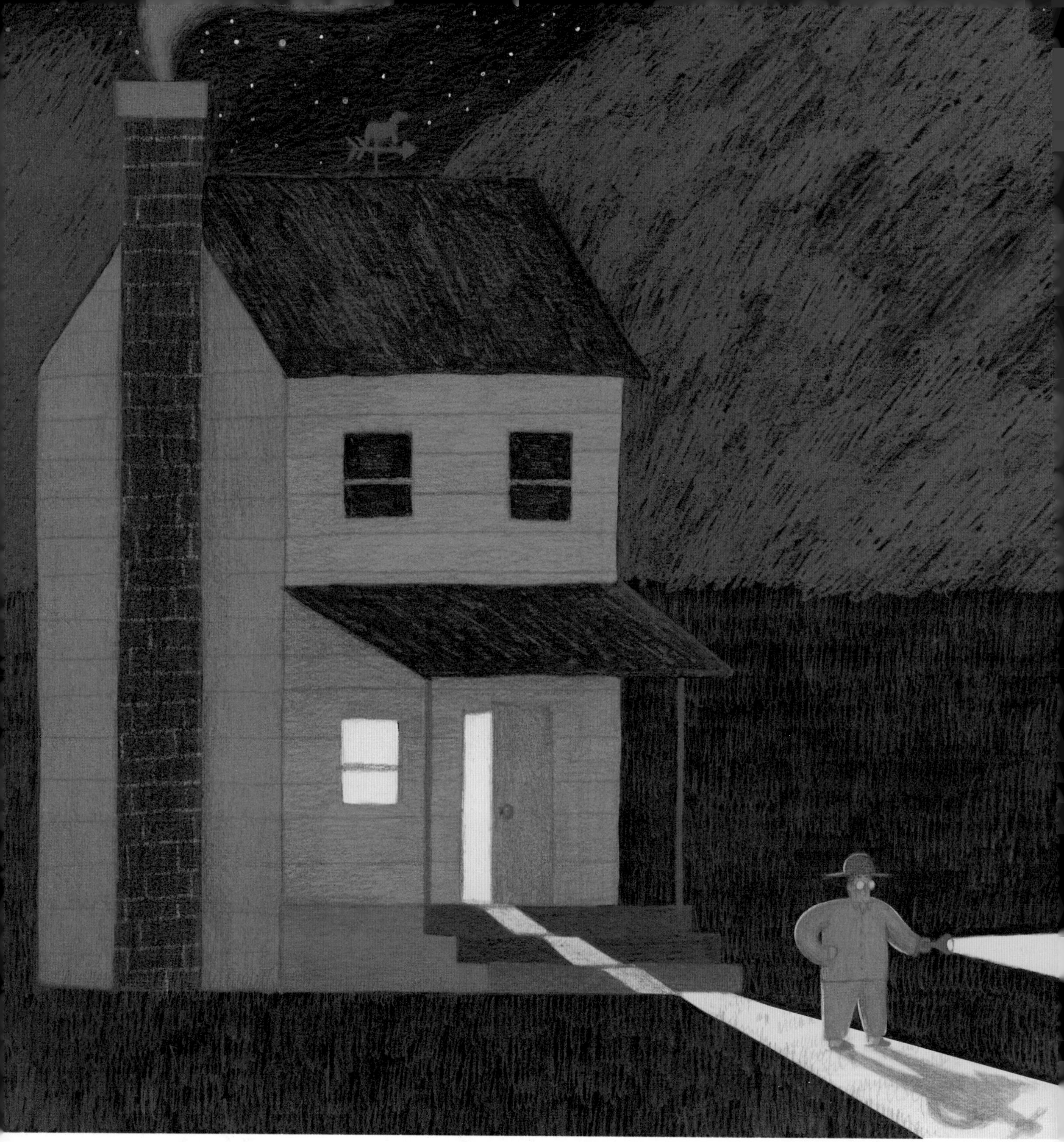

Mr. Li shined a flashlight into the dark night.

There was whispering and rustling
in the trees.

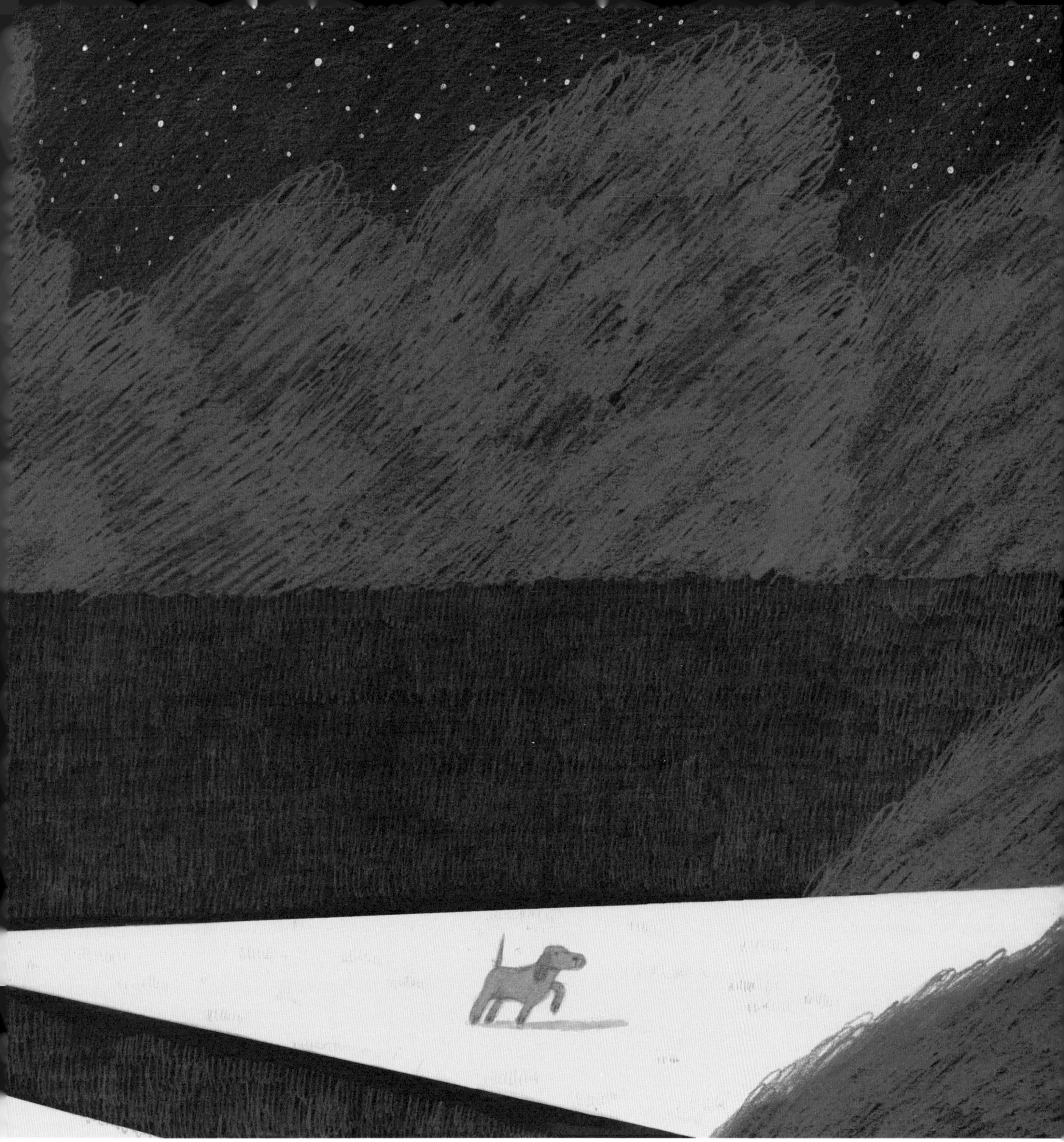

“Who’s there?!” he yelled.

And then three strangers appeared.

Their eyes were very big,
their skin was very blue
and their shape was very hard to describe.

"Hello," said the short one.
"We are DEFINITELY human."

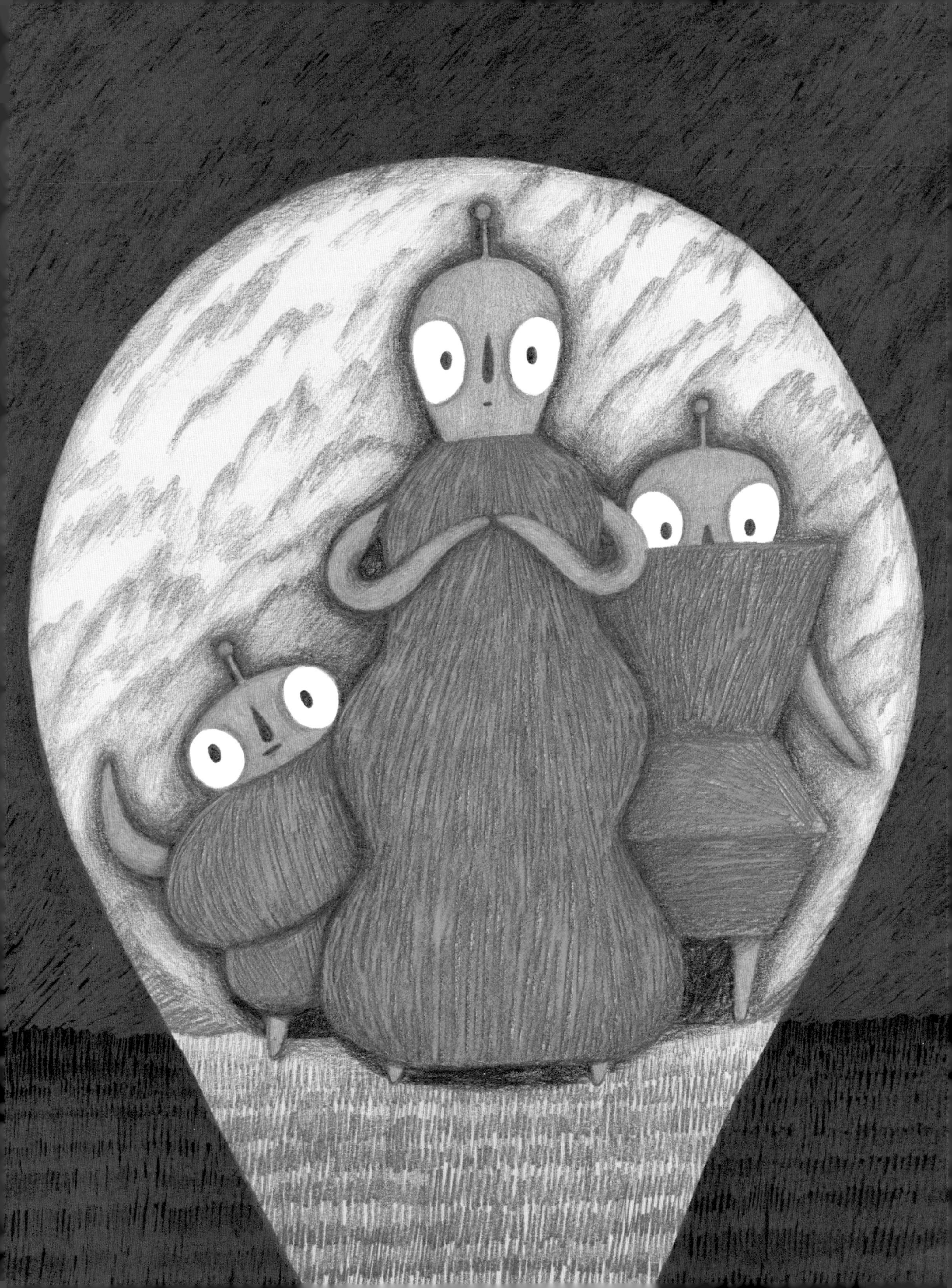

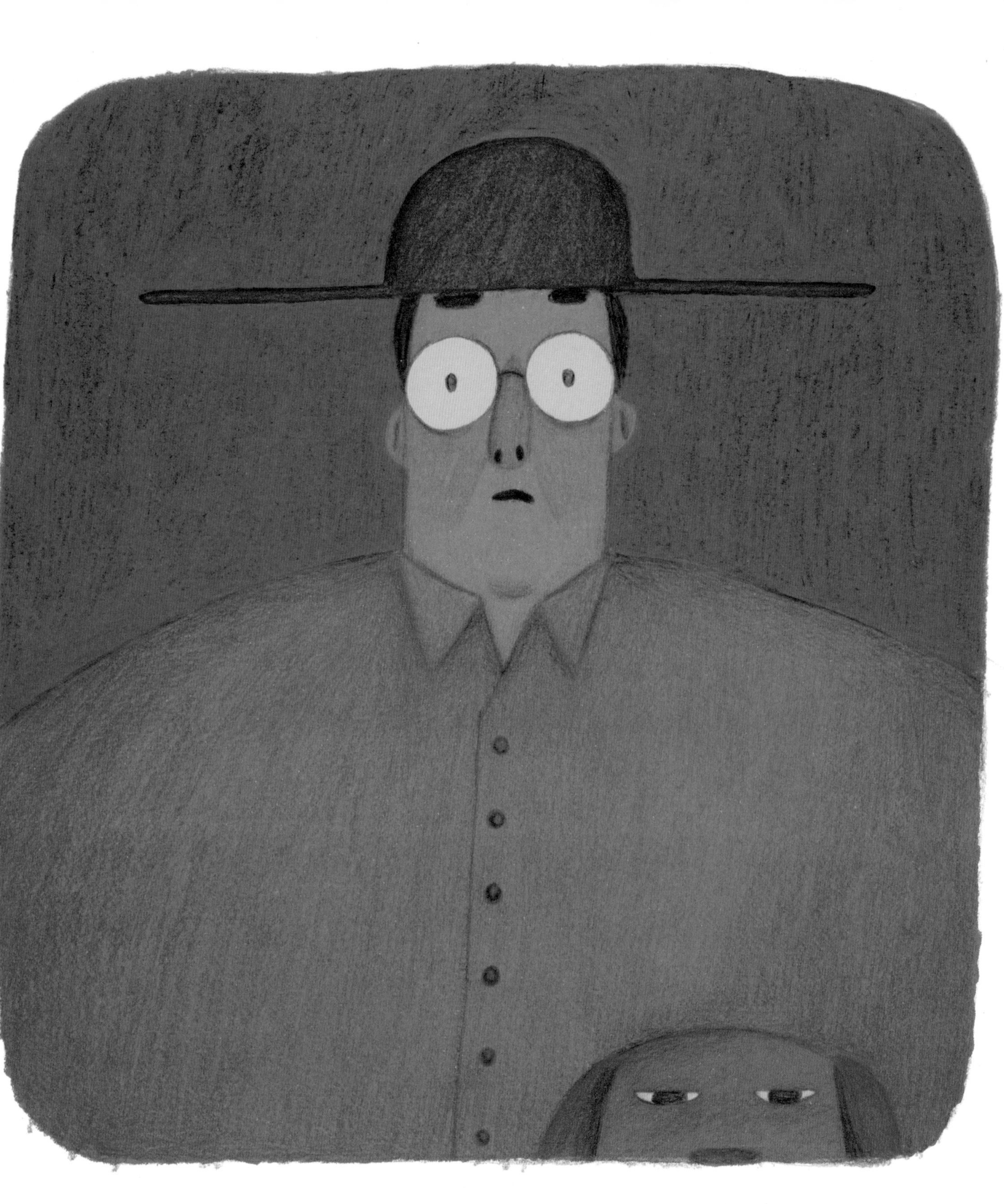

There was a long pause
as Mr. Li stared at the strangers.

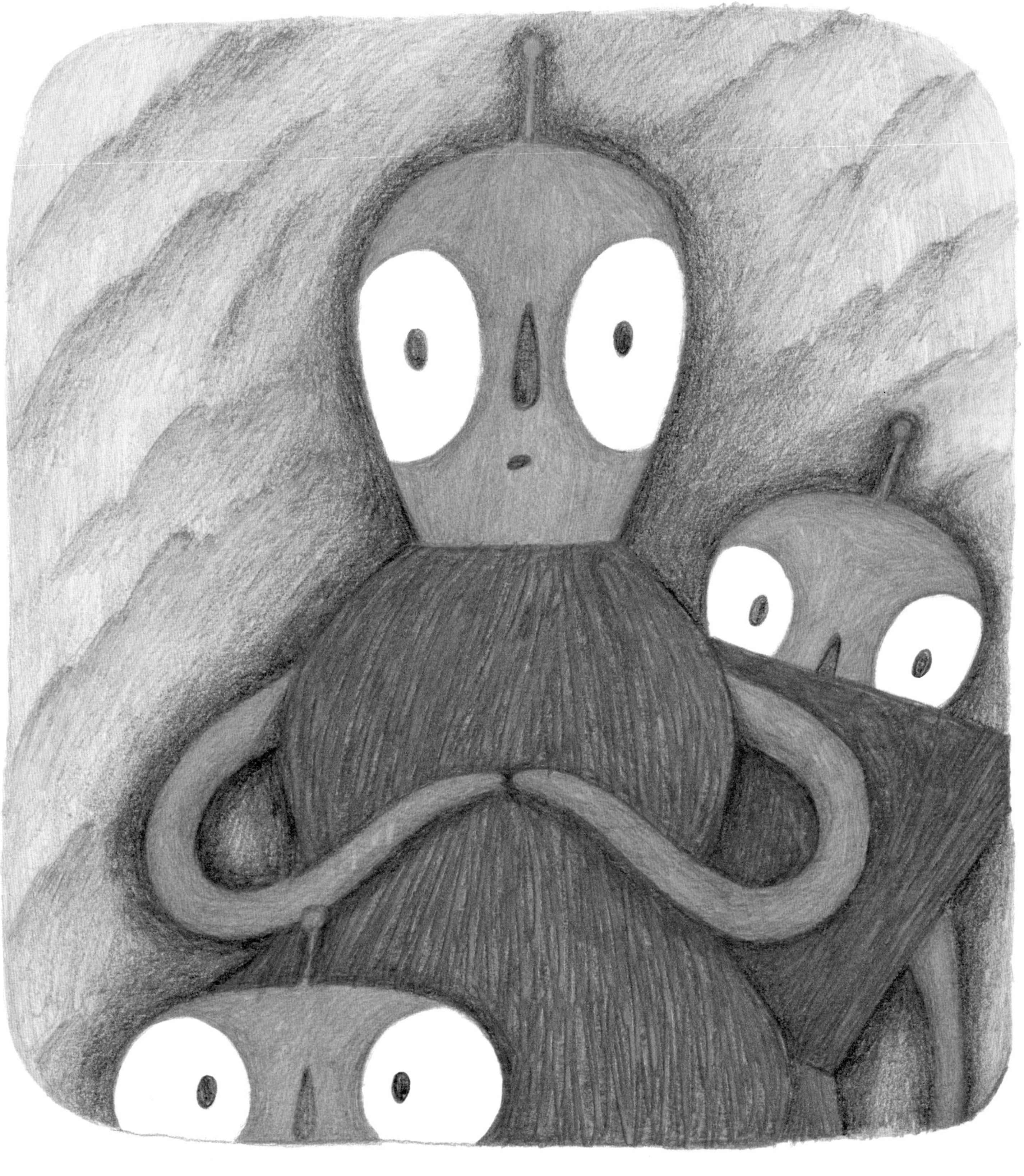

And the strangers stared back.

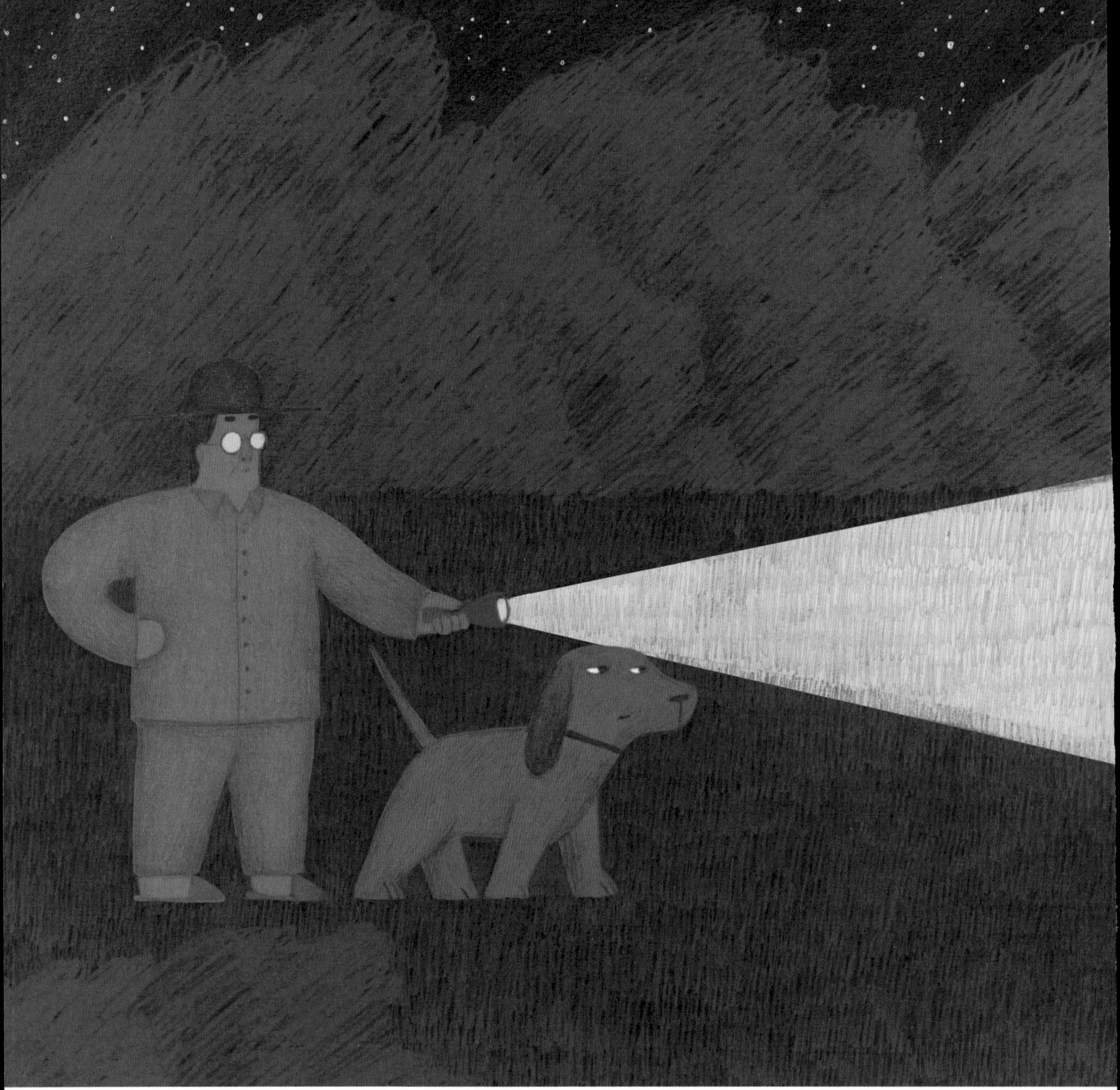

“Okay, if you say so,” Mr. Li finally replied. “But what are y’all doing here?”

“Our . . . car . . . broke down, and we need materials to fix it,” said the tall one.

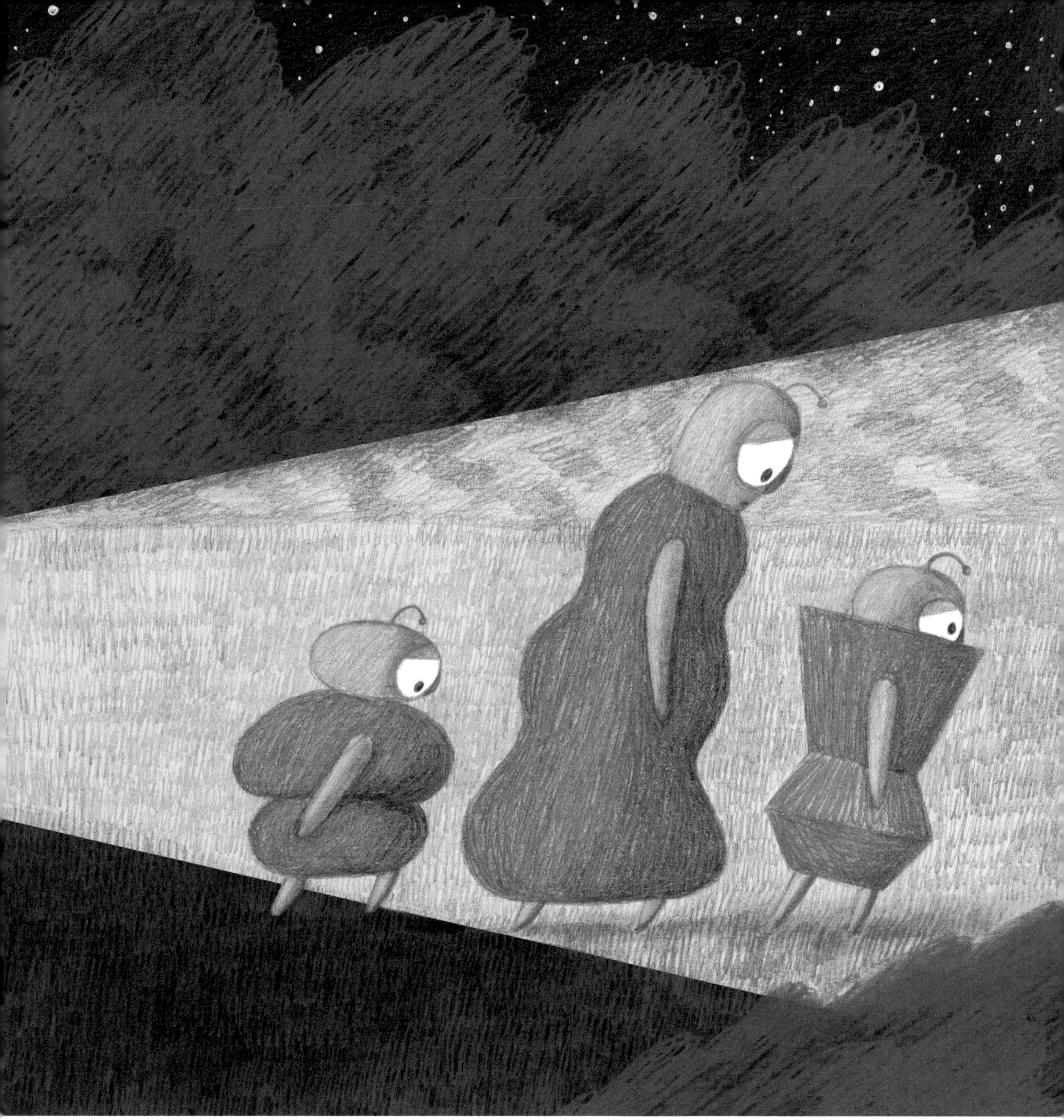

“It’s past midnight! There are no stores open now,” Mr. Li replied.

Disappointed, the three strangers turned to walk back into the dark night.

But Mr. Li was a kind human,
and he did what kind humans do.
He offered to help.

"Now wait a minute," he said,
"y'all can sleep in my house tonight.
We can go to the store tomorrow
and get what you need."

The strangers were surprised by this
kindness, but they happily accepted.

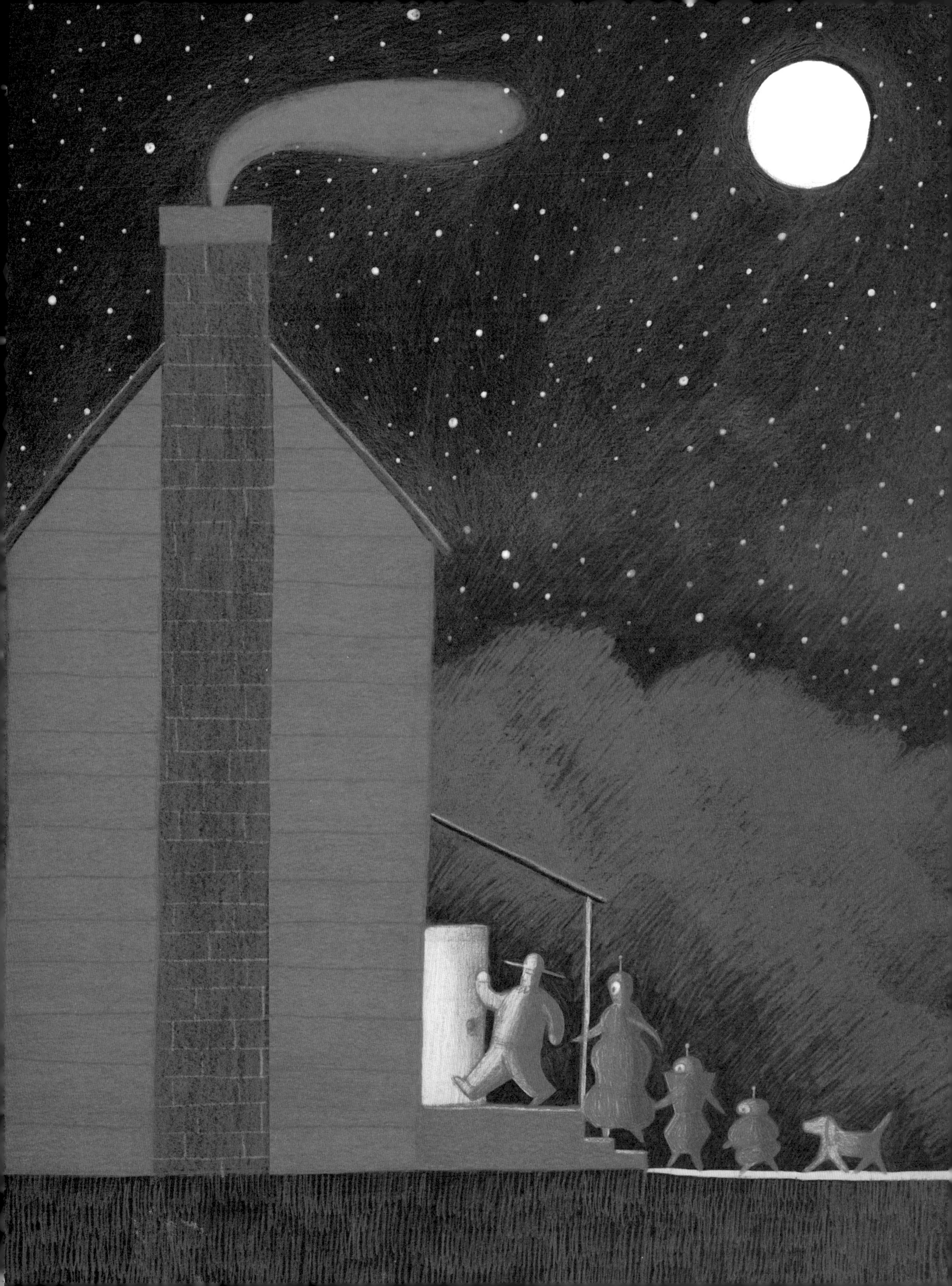

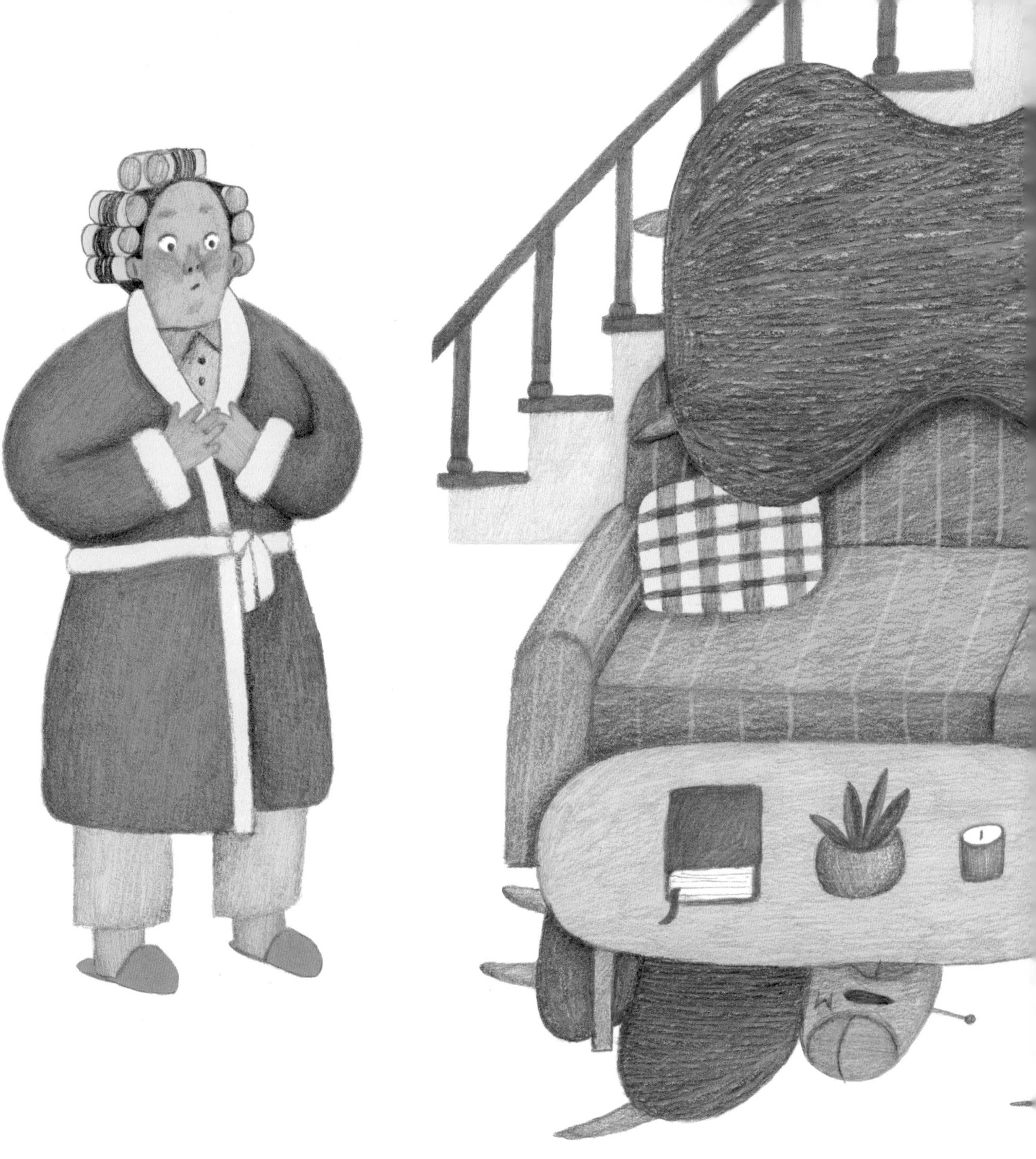

The next morning, Mrs. Li was surprised when she found three unexpected guests in her home.

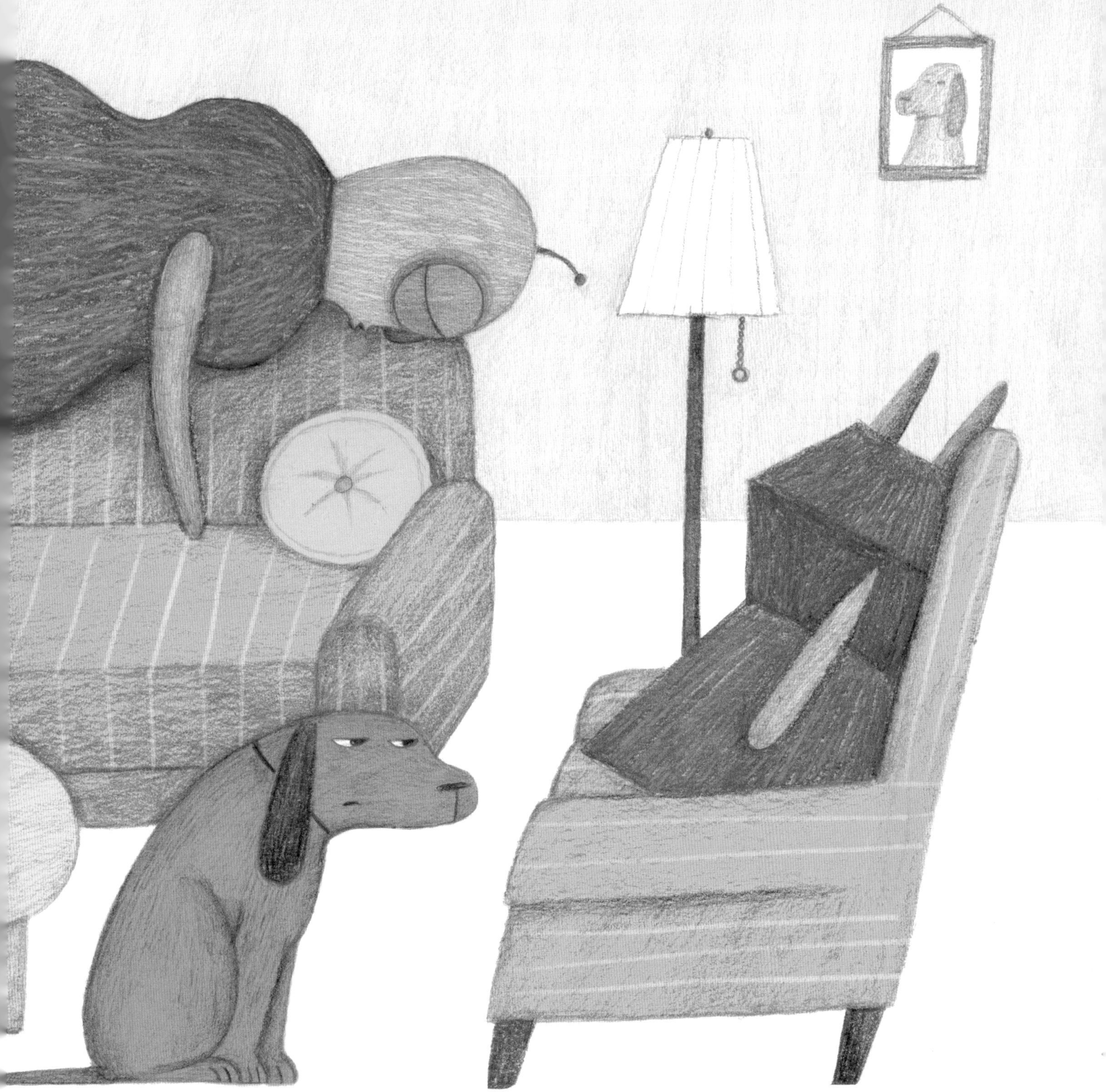

Mrs. Li found them somewhat odd.

"Now where are y'all from?" she asked.

"We are from . . . Europe," said the tall one.

"Oh. Okay!" said Mrs. Li.
"And what do y'all do in . . . *Europe*?"

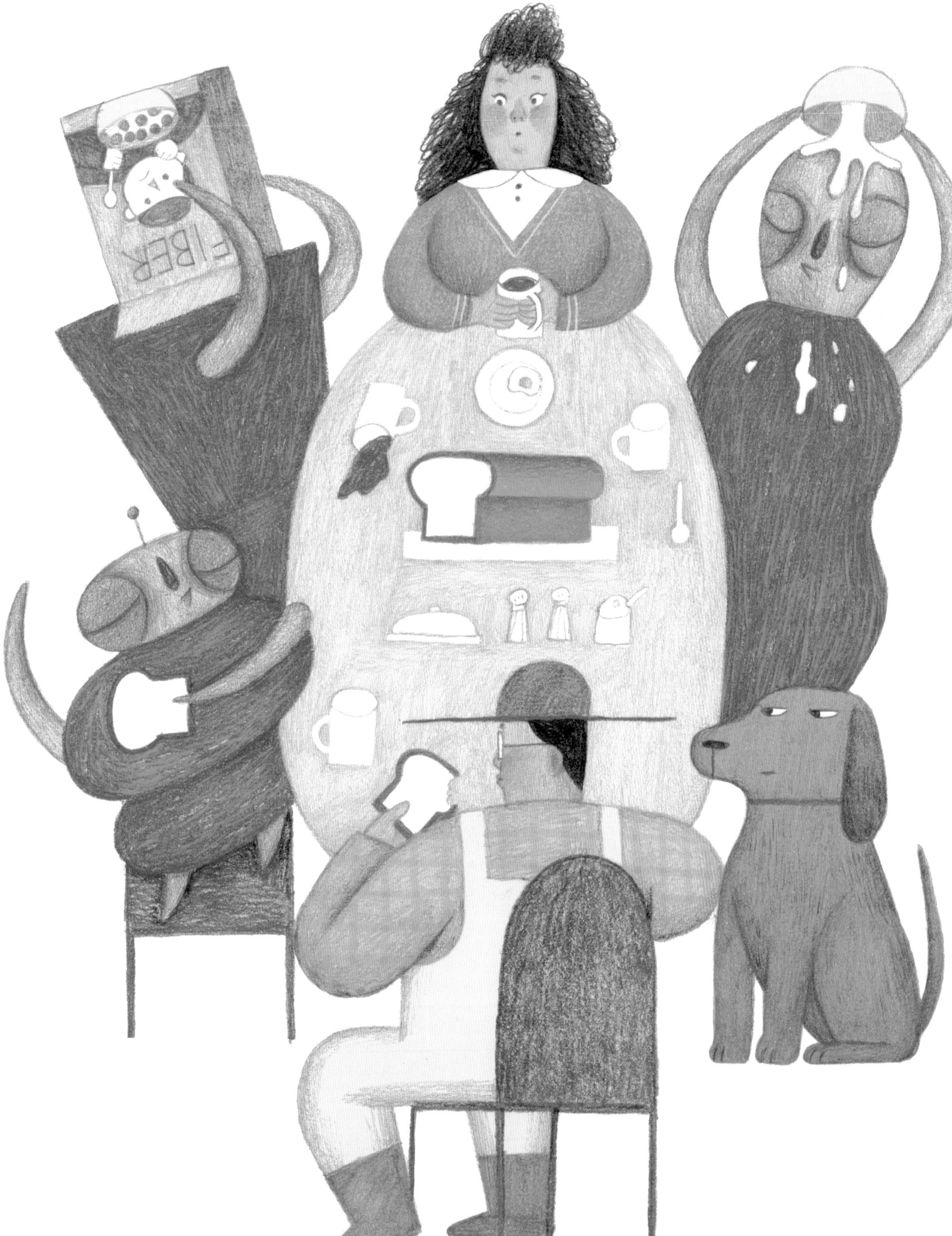
FIBER

"I make business,"
said the short one.

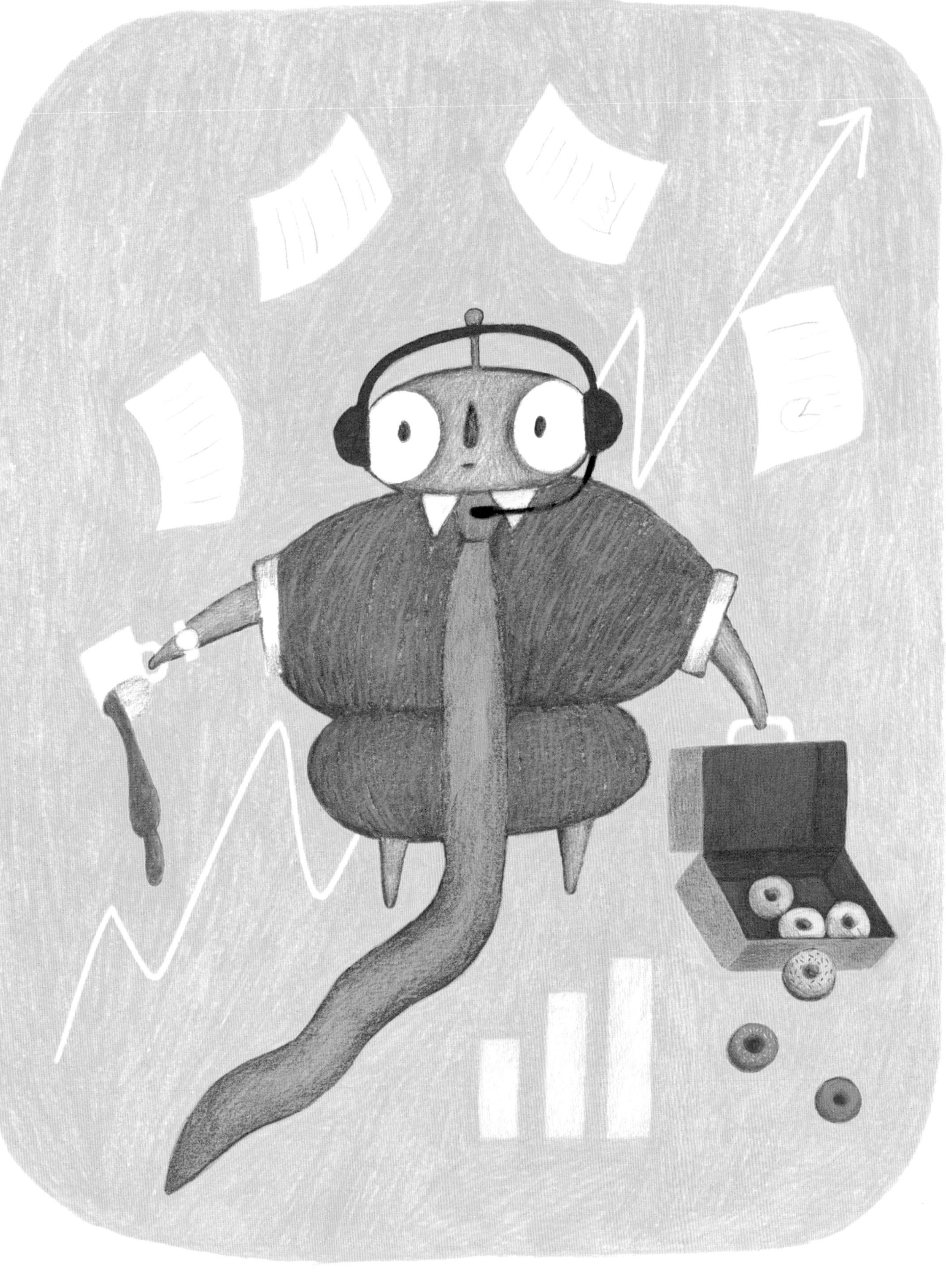

"I play sportsball,"
said the tall one.

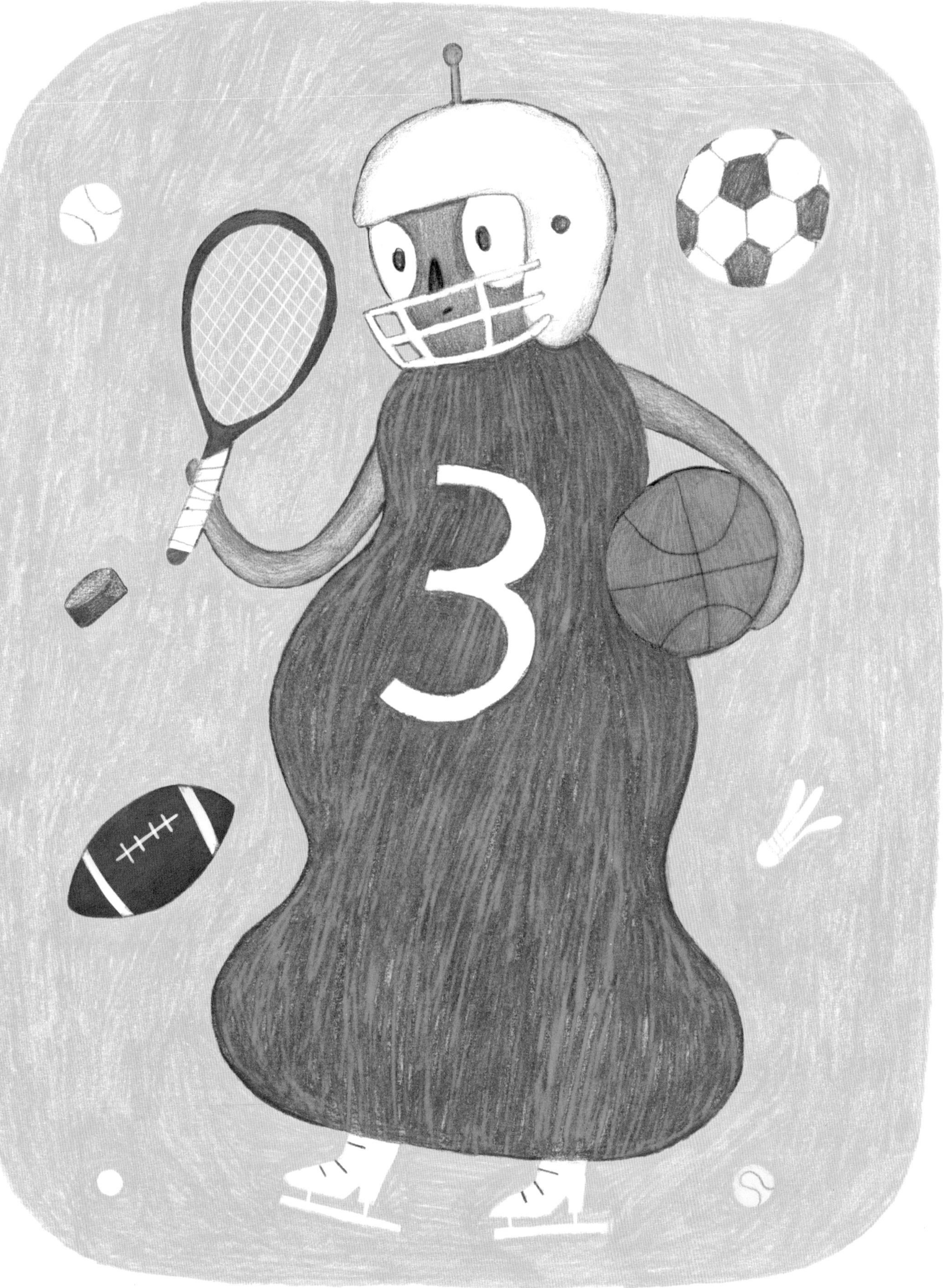
3

"I wear hat,"
said the one
wearing the hat.

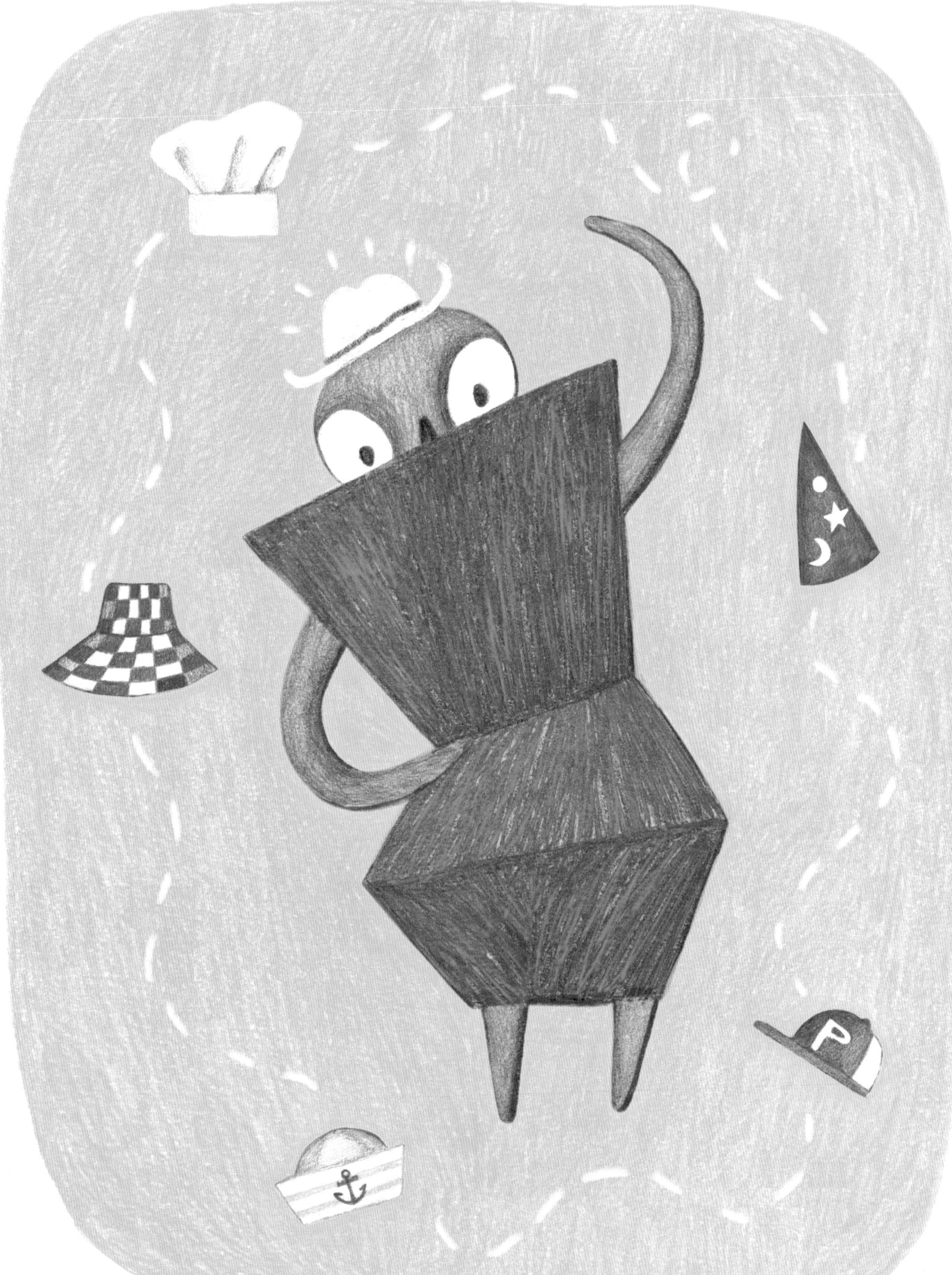

After breakfast,
Mr. Li drove his guests
to the store as promised.

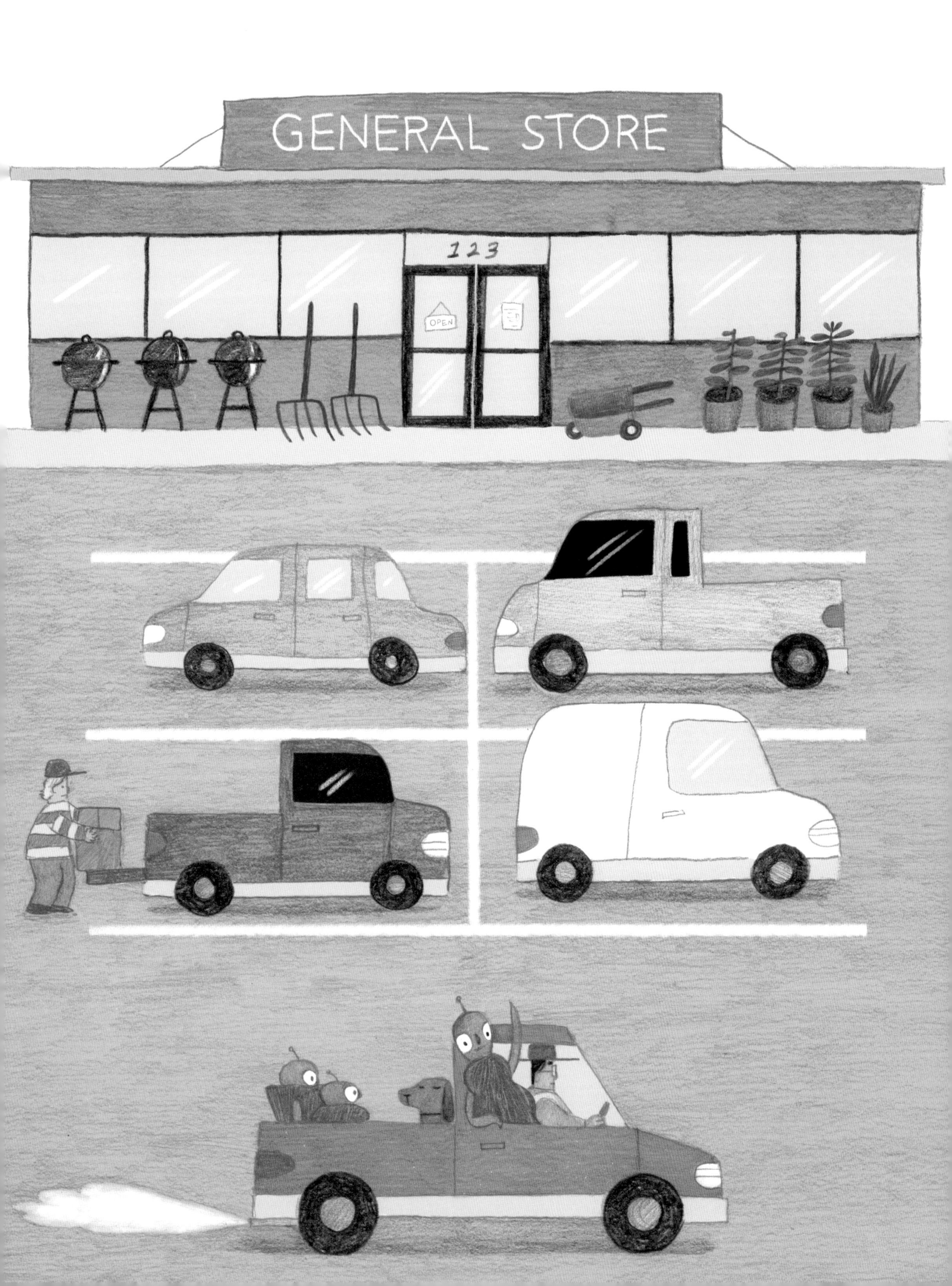
GENERAL STORE
123
OPEN

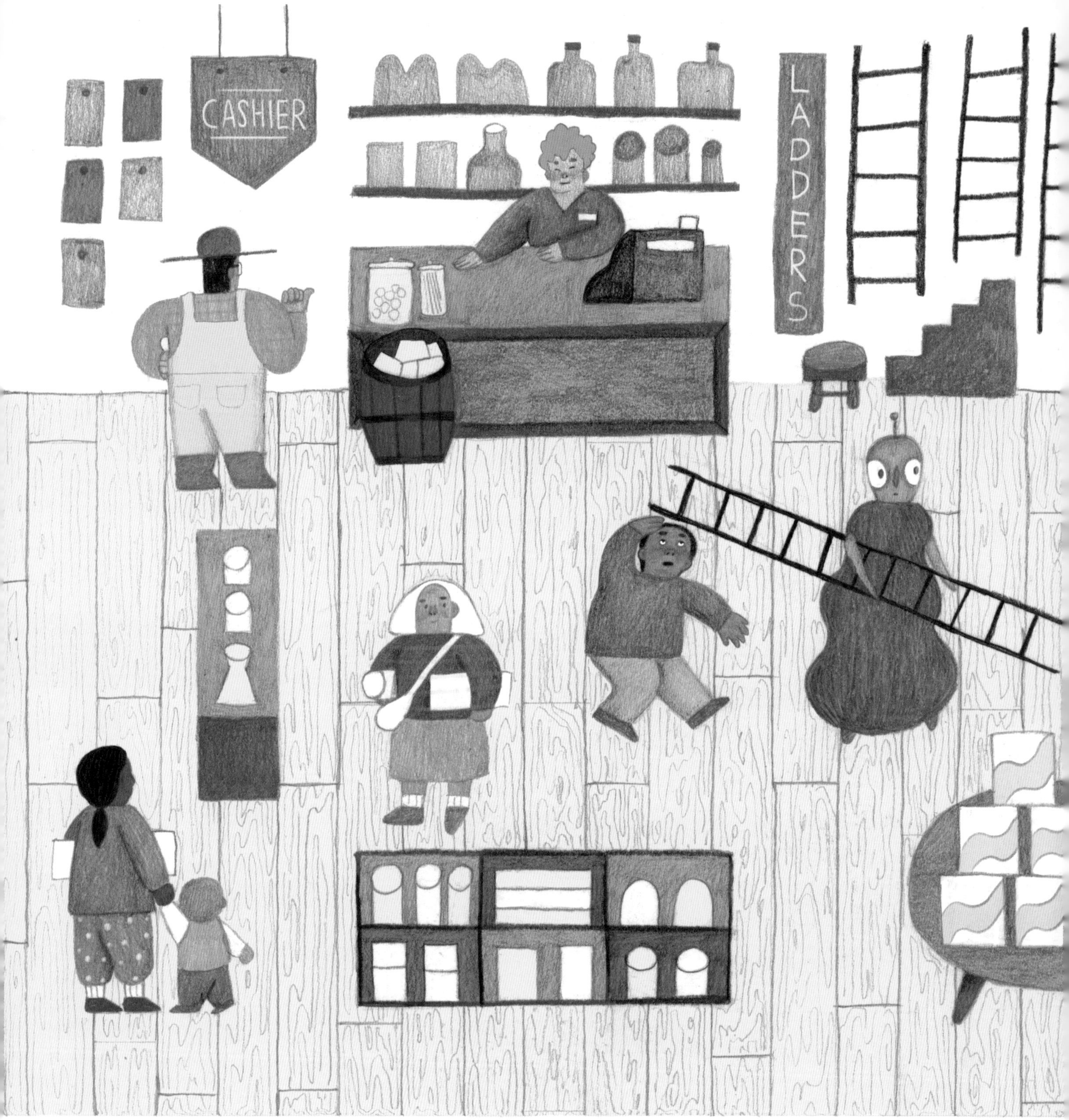
CASHIER
LADDERS

The people in the store thought there was something unique about the three visitors.

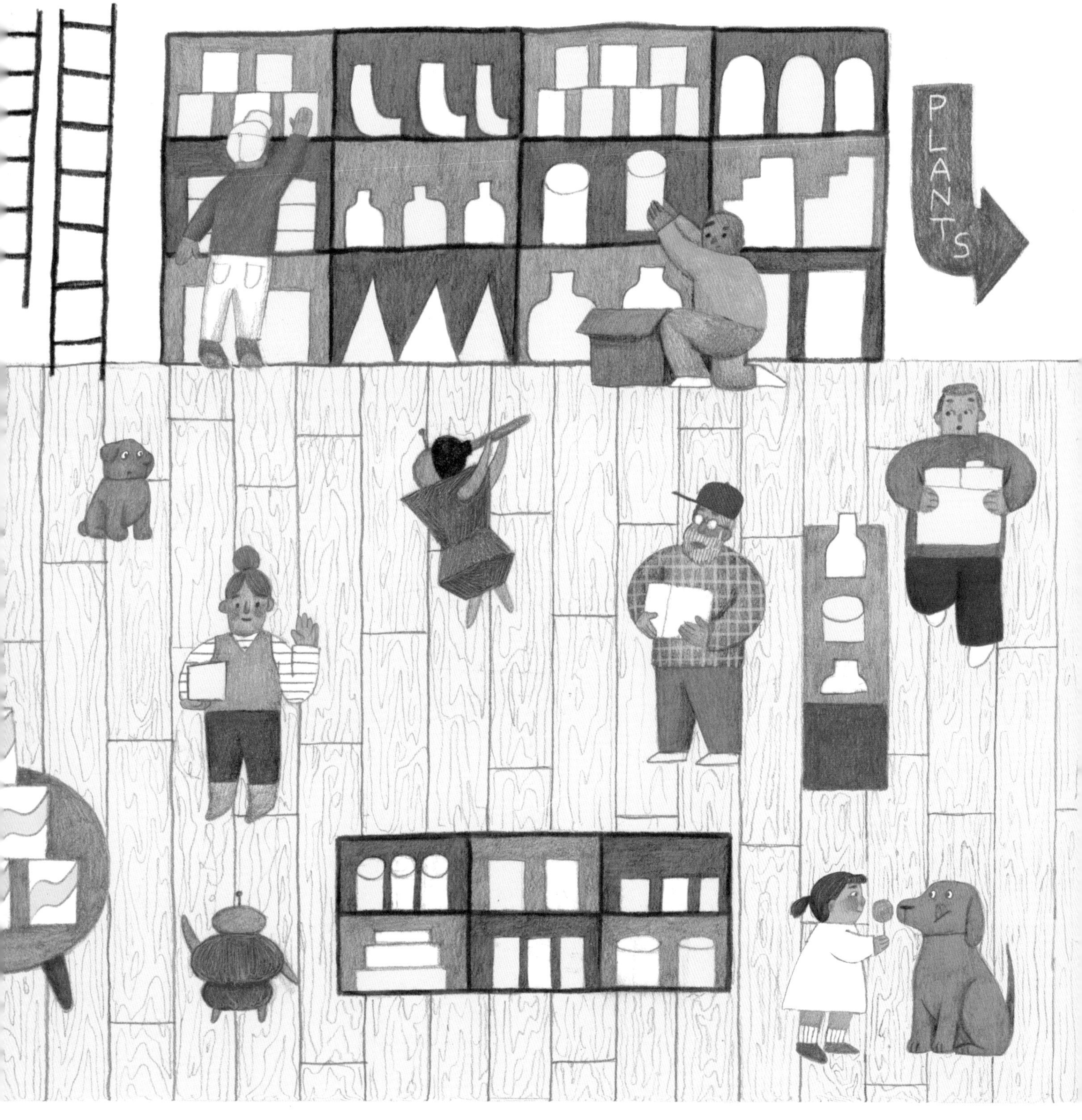
PLANTS

“Hello. We are DEFINITELY human,” announced the short one.

“They’re from *Europe*,” Mr. Li added.

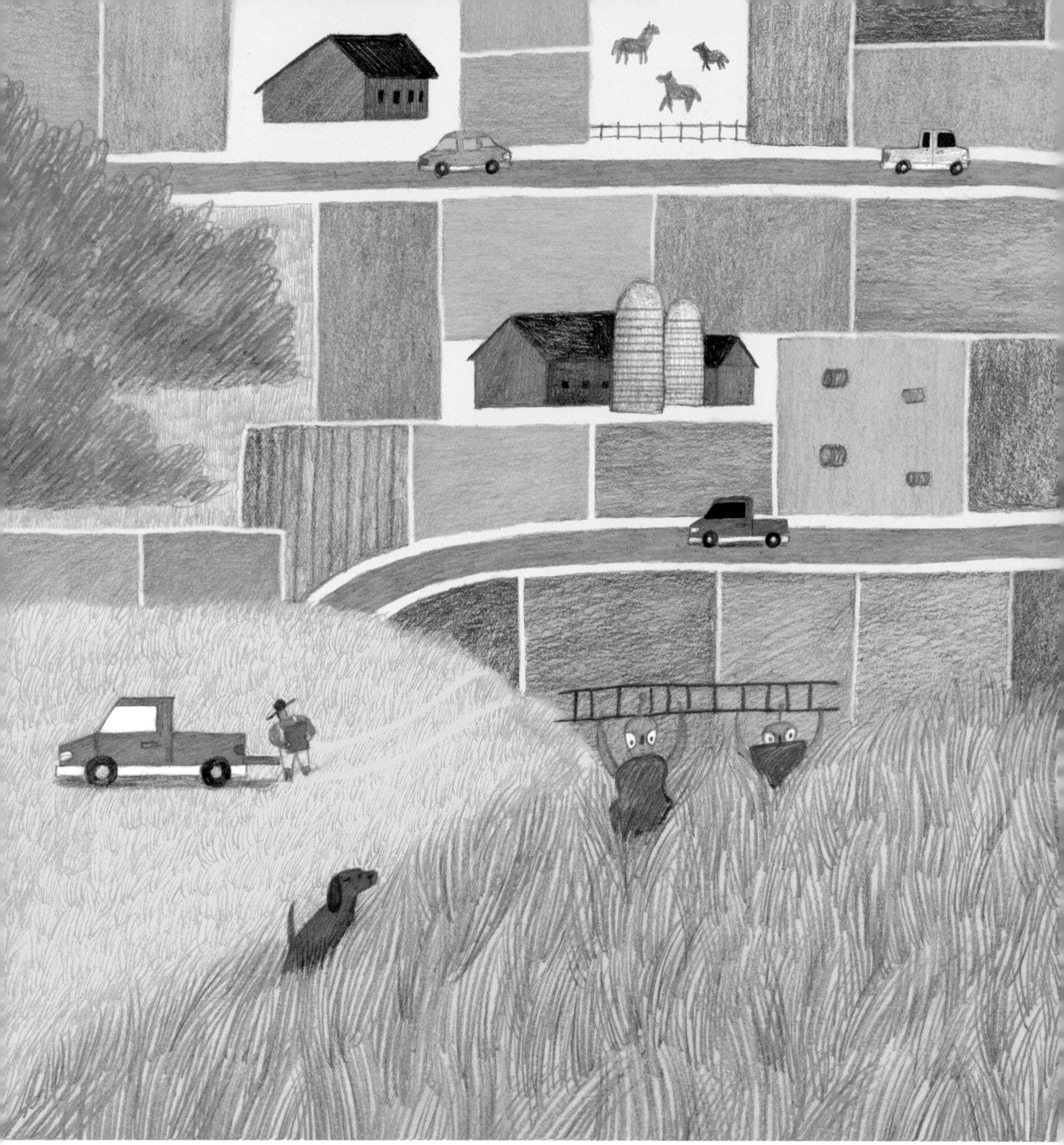

The people in the store were all kind humans, and they did what kind humans do.

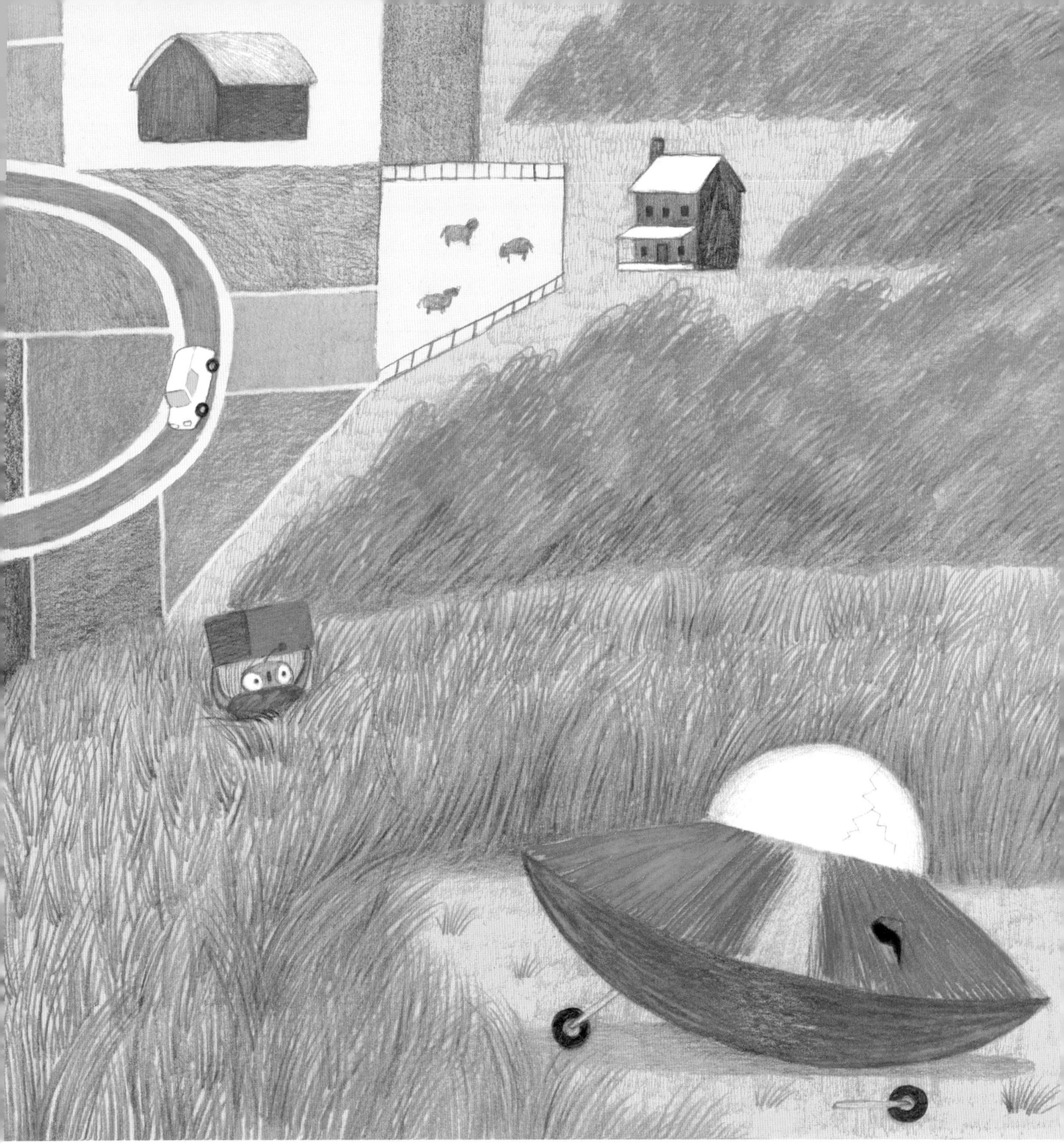

They offered to help the visitors fix their car.

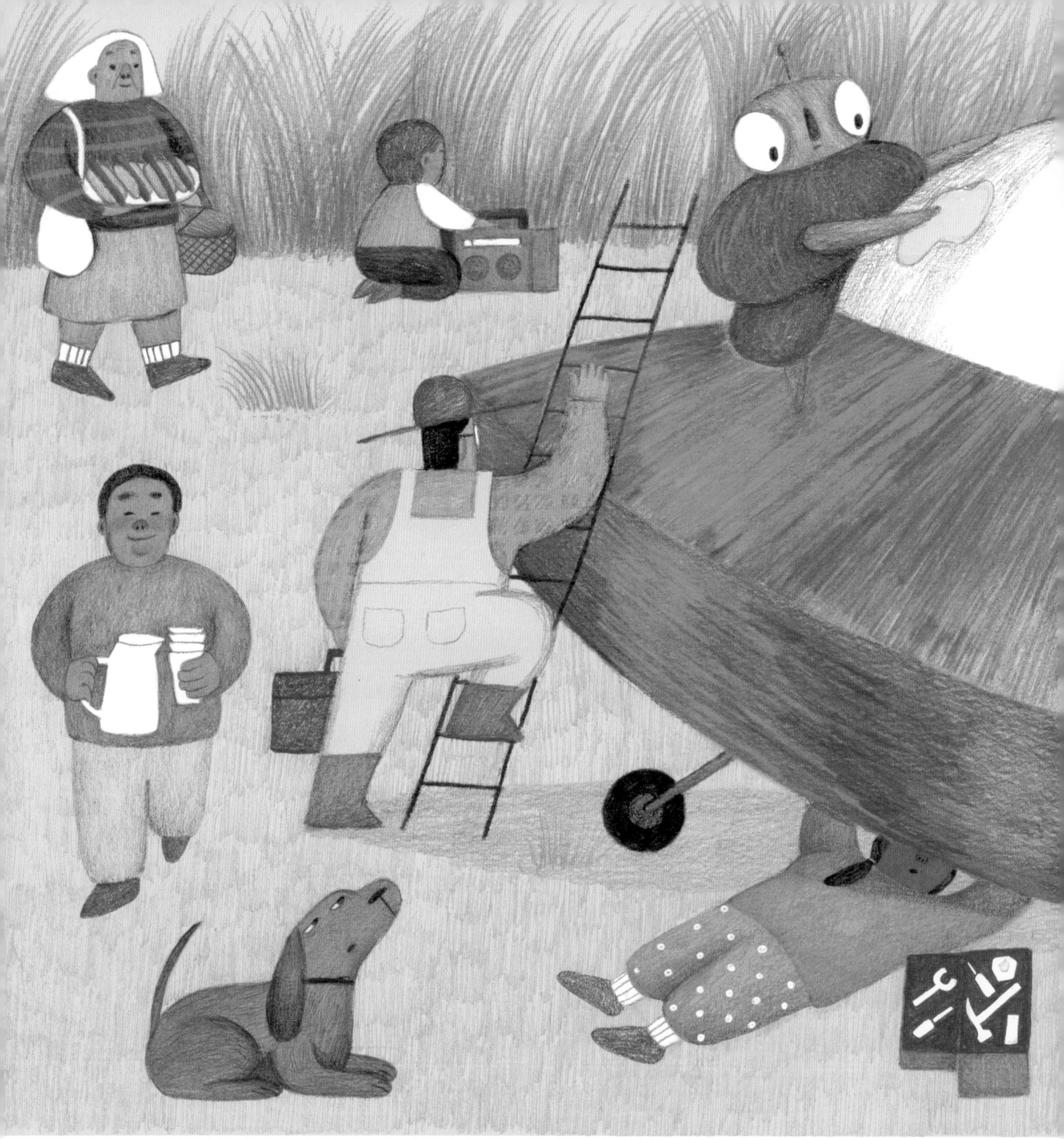

Some brought tools, others made food.
One person turned on a radio.

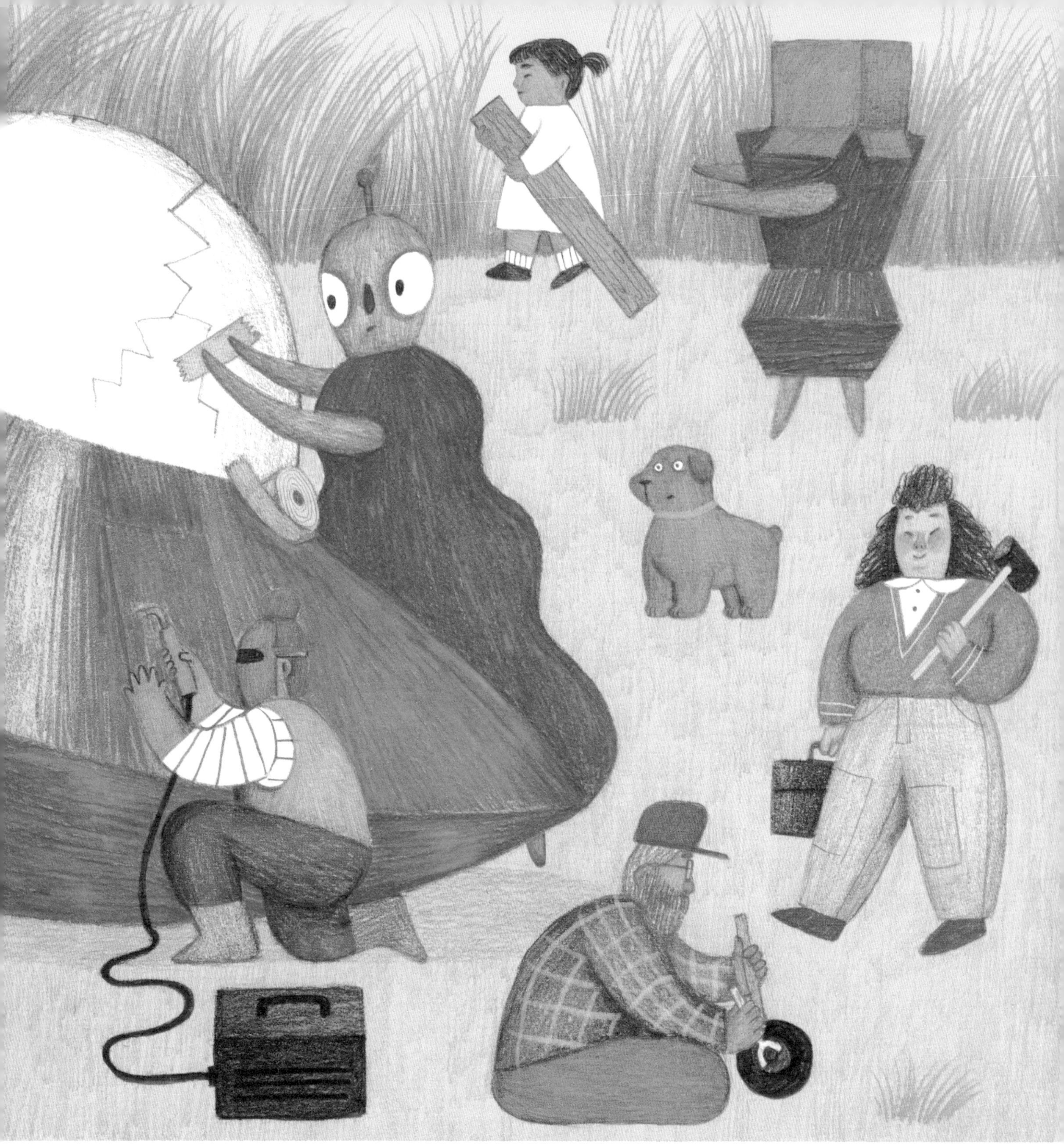

And before they knew it,
a little party had started.

There was dancing.

"Why are we moving our bodies like this?" asked the tall one.

"Because it's fun!" replied Mrs. Li.

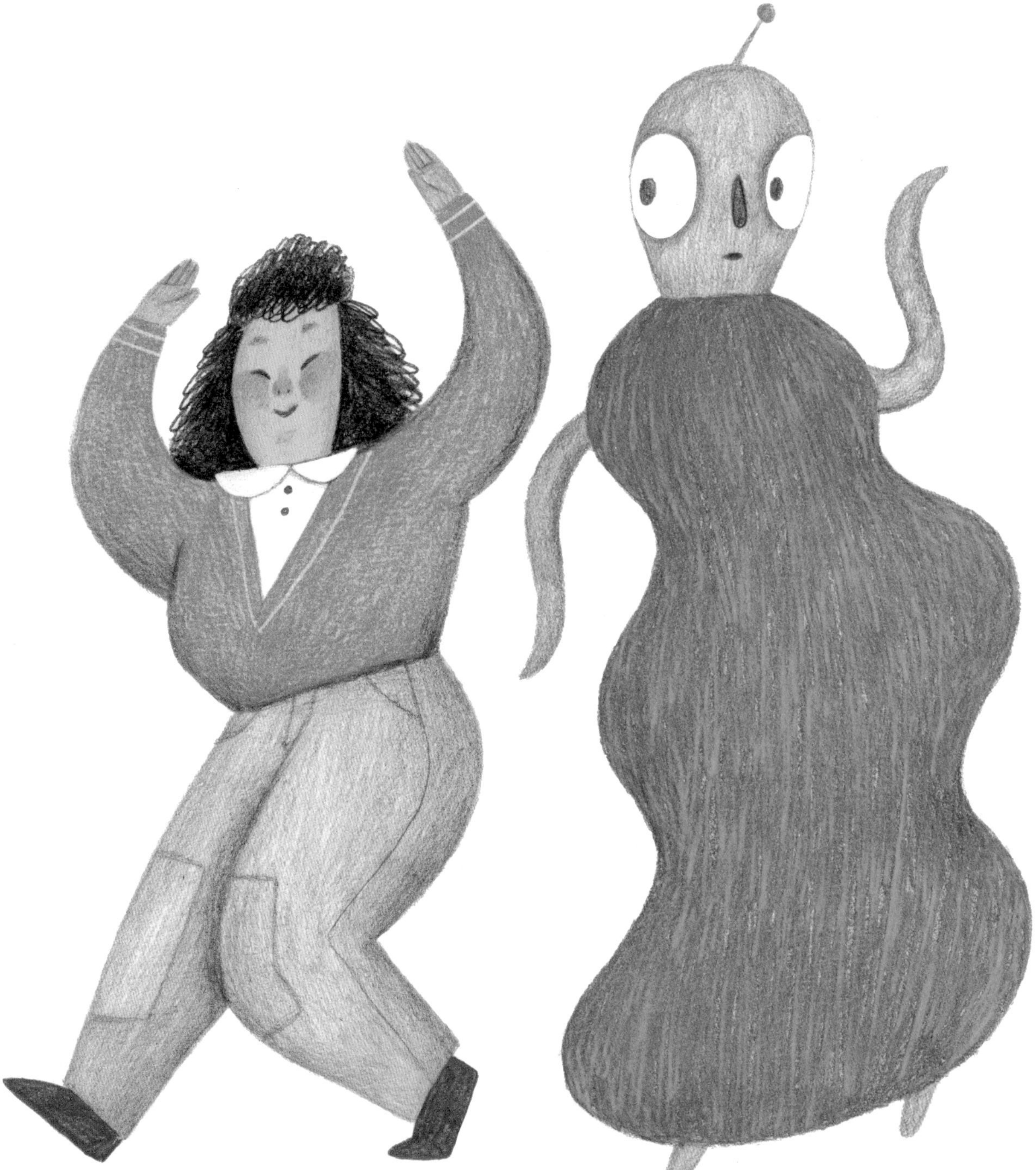

There was eating.

"Food goes into the *mouth*," explained Mr. Li.

And there were interesting conversations.

"Bark! Bark!" said the dogs.

"That's very interesting," replied the short one.

Finally, the car was fixed,
and it was time for the
three visitors to leave.

Everyone waved as their car
floated higher and higher until it
disappeared among the stars.

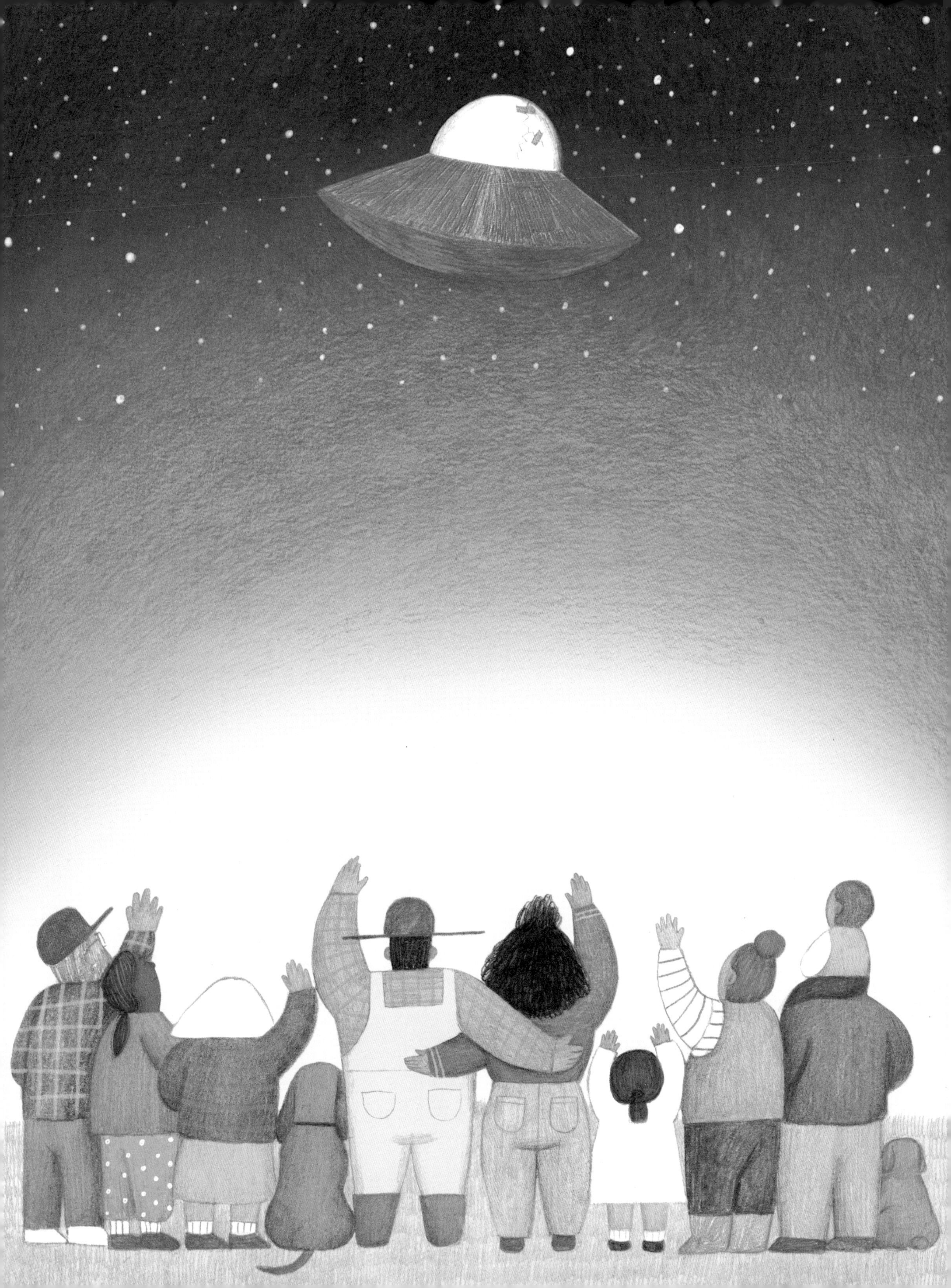

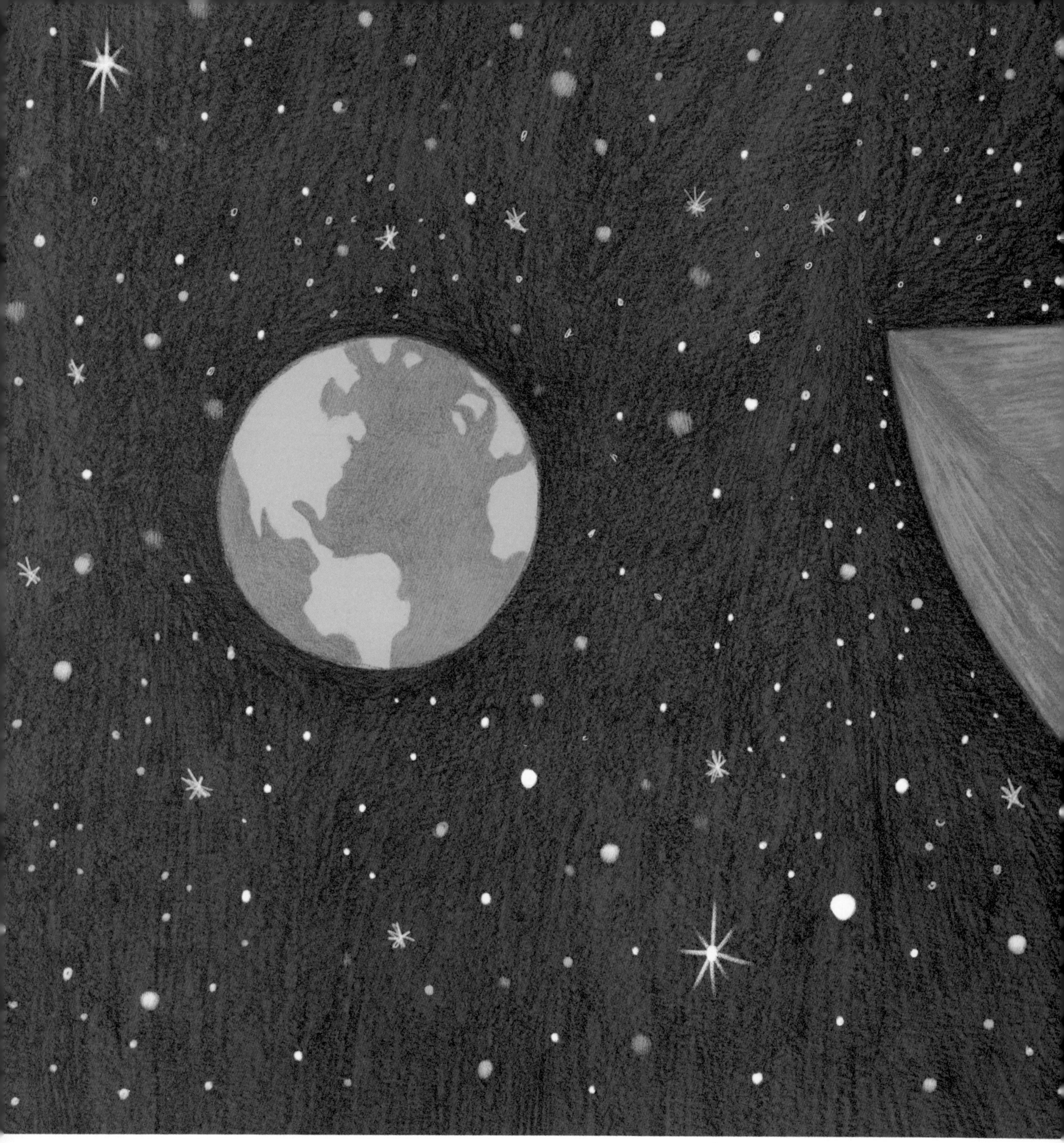

The three visitors continued
on their journey to far away places.

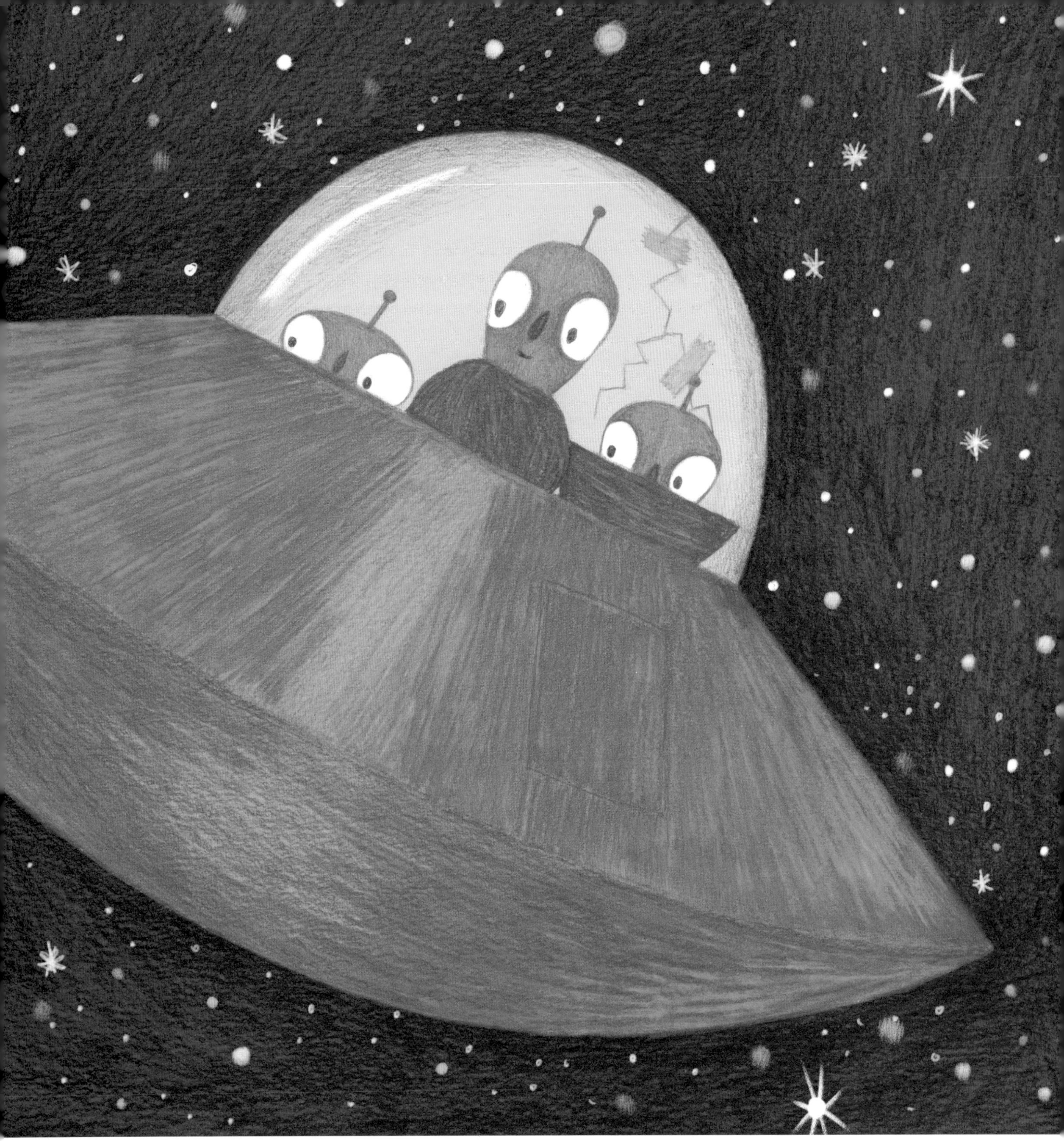

But wherever they went,
they would remember kind humans
and do what kind humans do —
offer help to those in need.

"Yep, they are DEFINITELY not from Europe."

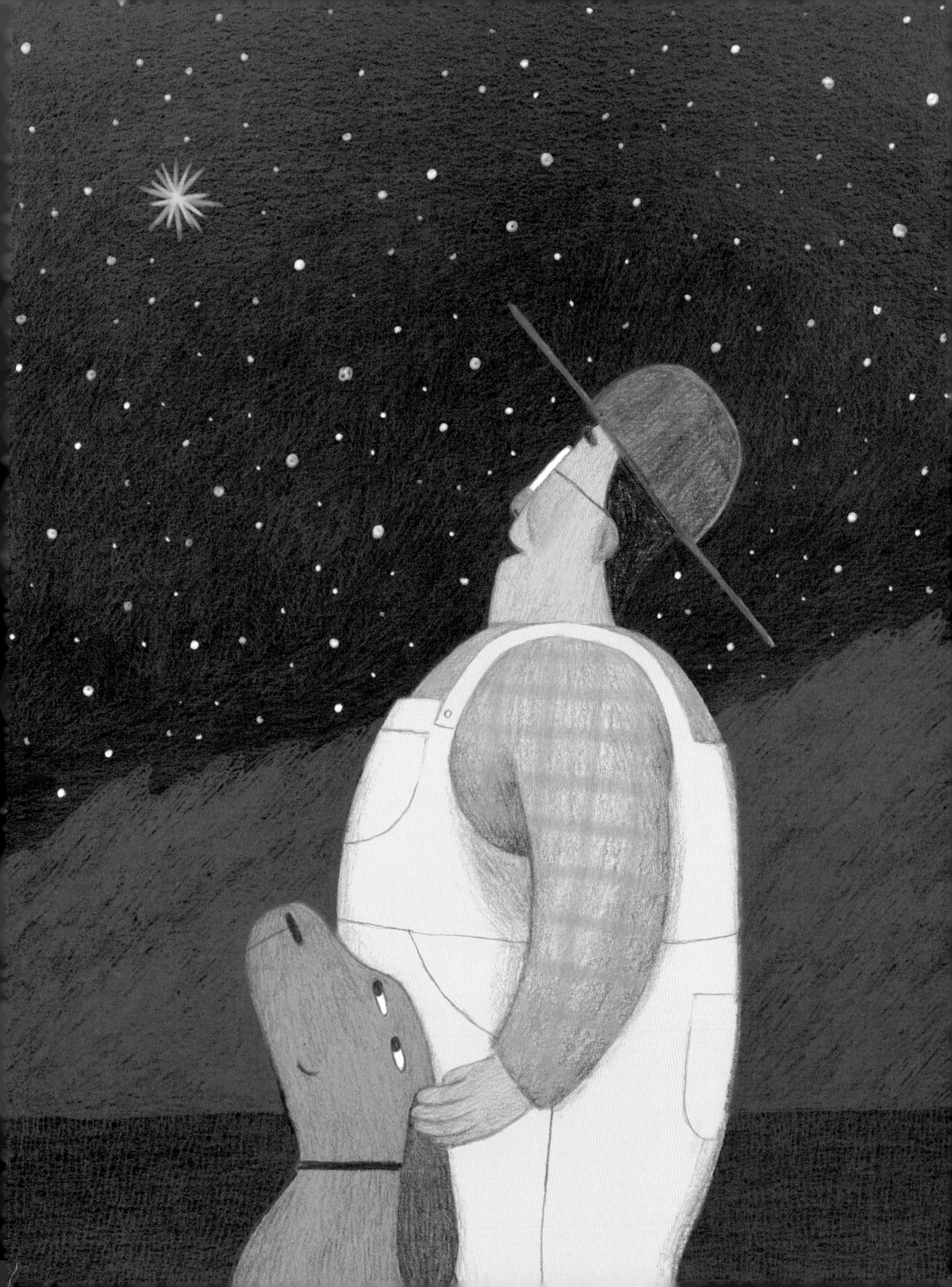

TO ALL THE KIND HUMANS

Tundra Books, an imprint of Tundra Book Group,
a division of Penguin Random House of Canada Limited

Library and Archives Canada Cataloguing in Publication

Title: We are definitely human / X. Fang.
Names: Fang, X., author, illustrator.
Identifiers: Canadiana (print) 20230485413 | Canadiana (ebook) 20230485421 |
ISBN 9781774882023 (hardcover) | ISBN 9781774882030 (EPUB)
Subjects: LCGFT: Picture books.
Classification: LCC PZ7.1.F36 W42 2024 | DDC j813/.6—dc23

Published simultaneously in the United States of America by
Tundra Books of Northern New York, an imprint of Tundra Book Group,
a division of Penguin Random House of Canada Limited

Library of Congress Control Number: 2023941987

Edited by Tara Walker with assistance from Ashley Rhamey
Designed by John Martz
The artwork in this book was created with
graphite pencil on paper and colored digitally.
The text was set in Century Schoolbook.

Printed in China

www.penguinrandomhouse.ca

1 2 3 4 5   28 27 26 25 24

Penguin
Random House
TUNDRA BOOKS